Swing Sets

Adriana Erin Rivera

Allie,

Thank you so much for coming to the signing! Enjoy the book!

ISBN: 150072727X
ISBN 13: 9781500727277

This is for all the forever-kids.

ACKNOWLEDGEMENTS

My friends inspired the humor of this novel. Their individual accounts of the struggles of post-graduation and, of course, the hilarious things they say helped me make this a project that I hope they can see a bit of themselves in.

I need to thank Colin Haynes for constantly motivating me to write more and finish this novel. Thank you for being my forever.

I am forever grateful to Professor Michael Hyde and Dr. Robert Clark for being so generous to set aside time from their busy schedules to review this novel and offer invaluable guidance that was immensely helpful in completing the writing of this novel.

My parents have always been the presidents of my fan club and my toughest critics. I appreciate all of the sacrifices they have had to make for me over the years. Without the inspiration of that swing set in our old backyard, this story would probably not exist. So I have to thank them for getting that for me and everything they do for me.

Table of Contents

CHAPTER ONE

"The beginning is the most important part of the work." – Plato

The realization hit me as soon as I woke up. It was my 21st birthday. The 27th of June possessed the capability to turn the fate of this bright and sunny day into a dream or a nightmare.

My mother called out from the kitchen for me to come downstairs to eat breakfast. So I pulled the covers over and attempted sitting up. It was a sleeping morning. As hard as I tried reaching my arms out, the sitting up part would not happen. Then, I tried the rollover approach and leaned to my right, little by little, until I made a big thump sound on the floor.

"Ugh," I muttered under my breath.

That seemed to wake me up and I promptly jumped back up. I walked over to my vanity and looked at myself up close in the mirror. I was 21. I was officially an adult. I was an adult who could legally drink, an adult who could finally take on responsibilities, but most importantly, I was an adult who had freedom. Finally, I pulled my long black hair into a tight ponytail, took one last look in the mirror motioning an *I'm looking at you* gesture at my reflection jokingly, and swiftly opened my bedroom door as if to say, "Here I am world! I'm an adult! Hear me roar!"

I began slowly sauntering down the stairs to make a grand birthday entrance, but upon smelling the glorious pancakes my mother was flipping in the kitchen, I ran down instead.

"Mmm! ¡*Panqueques!*" I said as I bee-lined it to my chair at the table.

"Happy birthday, Josefina," my mother said as she set my pancake-filled plate on the table and kissed me on the head.

Across from my seat was my father reading the newspaper straight in front of his face.

"Ah, *Felíz Cumpleaños!*" he said from behind the façade of the newspaper. "21 years young, eh?" he continued with a chuckle.

I shot a glance at my mom, who simply shrugged off his response. He seemed to be almost mocking my birthday as if it symbolized something I hadn't quite figured out yet.

"Thanks, Dad," I settled for a quick answer rather than participate in whatever mind puzzle he had in store for me. My father always loved puzzles. When I was younger, my dad bought me a book of mind puzzles and assigned certain pages for me to solve. He said they would make me smarter. However, all I wanted were the delicious-looking chocolate chip pancakes that were sitting in front of me just waiting to be eaten. There was no time for mind puzzles.

As I started eating my pancakes, my father decided to make conversation with me about my birthday plans. Now let's be clear about something: I love my dad. He taught me how to ride a bike and not wipe out, and shoot a basketball and actually make it in the basket. My dad is boss, but he's also the boss of everything in our house. He's actually a lawyer so he makes the rules around here.

"Are you planning on going out tonight with anyone?" he asked, still behind the newspaper.

I answered that with an, "I don't know yet," and took a sip of my orange juice.

"Not even Bethany?" he persisted with this topic.

I repeated with emphasis, "I don't know yet."

"Do you have any plans for today?"

"Not really," I said as I stuffed a huge chunk of pancakes in my mouth. Then, I inquired, "Why do you ask?" with a full mouth and chipmunk cheeks. I knew I would regret that question as soon as those words left my mouth.

My dad lowered his newspaper shield and set it down on the table in between us. "I have a project I think you might find interesting."

I uttered a barely audible and skeptical, "uh huh," in response. I knew he had something up his sleeve! I knew it. There was no way I was going to get through my 21st birthday unscathed.

"Think of this as a research project. Yes! That's exactly what it is – a research project."

Another, "uh huh," was my response to that part. I figured the less I said, the easier it would be to get out of whatever project this might be.

Then, my dad vigorously flipped through the newspaper. I wasn't sure what he was searching for so I just continued drinking my O.J.

"Ah!" my father resounded over finding what he was looking for with such fervor. He twisted the newsprint toward my direction so I could read it.

"The classifieds section?" I asked innocently. "What's this? This is the project?" I keenly took another swig of orange juice.

"You're going to find a job," my dad said point blank. "A real job," he specified. "A career job," he specified further.

I almost spat out my juice all over the newspaper – not because I didn't want to find a job, but the sheer thought that I had any actual job skills was laughable. So that's what I did. I laughed.

"This isn't funny, Josefina. You're an educated young woman. You are certainly capable of getting a job in your field."

I abruptly stopped laughing. "Yeah, but dad –"

"Yeah, but dad what? Josefina, this is not negotiable. Your mother and I think you need to really be an adult now and get a job. Something you can be proud of. Something you can earn money at."

Then, my mother joined in. "Sweetheart, you're an adult now with a college degree. You went to Princeton!"

I went to Princeton University after graduating high school a year early. In all my four years at Princeton, I never once lived on campus. I commuted from home. It was a little unconventional for me to commute to this particular campus, but I did it because my parents thought I would be safer at home – with them. They have always been a teensie bit overprotective and therefore I had been very sheltered and also never had a real job. I had been our neighbor's babysitter a few times. When I was in Girl Scouts, I volunteered at an old people home. I got a badge for it. That experience made me realize I really don't like dealing with old people. I'm no good at it. I'm not particularly good at anything other than studying.

Back to the breakfast table: my father made declarative statements. My mother smiled and nodded as her way to help make me feel less attacked by the whole situation.

"Just try, Josefina," my father said. "Make an effort in this."

"This will be a good thing for you," my ever-optimistic mother said sweetly. "It's part of growing up."

My head was spinning at this point. I couldn't get a word in edge-wise. This became a conversation of my parents with my face. There was no reaction in my eyes or anything. Stunned would be an under-statement of how I felt at that moment. I wasn't given a single second to process this "project," which meant that I couldn't conjure up an educated, adult response. I was an *adult*, after all.

So I did the only thing I knew how to do. I placed my head face down on the table and covered my head with my arms and stayed very still. It was almost like playing dead, but this way was much more comfortable than the not breathing way. It basically just confuses the attackers – in this case, my parents – so they eventually stop attacking you. I saw it in a movie once. And it worked. Silence. *Perfecto.*

My parents sat at the kitchen table waiting for me to react to some-thing. After a few minutes of blankly staring directly at the tabletop without a single helpful thought, I lifted my head, sat up, stood, and walked over to the screen door ahead on my line of sight that led straight to the backyard. I opened the door, walked on the grass in my bare feet and pajamas and headed for my swing set.

I actually liked to call it my swing-set-jungle-gym-apparatus. I've also always been very particular about how I sit on the swings. The swing on the right, from the sitting angle, was mine. I never swing on the left side. It may sound silly, but that's the way I would do things on my swing-set-jungle-gym-apparatus.

So I took my seat on the right side swing and kicked off. I was able to swing there for a few minutes while my parents were surely devising a plan to suddenly change everything about my life. On my swing-set-jungle-gym-apparatus, for once, I was able to think for myself.

It wasn't that I didn't want to get a job. I had just graduated a month ago with a degree in the Classics with a focus in Philosophy. As far as I knew, the only career path in that field was to be a college professor. I didn't want to be a professor. It sounded so boring to me. I wasn't going to let that be an option. However, I wasn't actually qualified for any other career path. I had no business being a doctor. Blood and guts really grossed me out. I could barely handle paper cuts. Perhaps I could do research of some sort. I could be a researcher if only I knew about the technical side of research. I was used to simply printing out the research results or taking a trip to the library, and then writing a paper on whatever research I found. Again – not professionally qualified. What was I supposed to do with a degree in the Classics *and* Philosophy? It was like a double whammy Jeopardy question.

Just as I was gaining optimal height and speed on my swing, my parents walked out to the backyard. My mother stood with her hands on her hips. Her left hand held a newspaper and her right hand held a red pen. My father stood with his arms crossed waiting for me to slow down and come back down to land. Truth was that I loved being up in the air with the wind in my hair and the breeze between my toes. That was my sublime time. I was untouchable – at least until my feet touched the ground again. If I had my choice, I would never stop swinging. That's the only place I could feel free. But alas, the swing was failing me and my feet felt the grass again. That meant I would have to face my parents. Cue the dark-doom music. I took a deep breath.

My mother started. "You need to take this seriously. You can't be dependent on us for the rest of your life. Don't you want to be an independent adult?"

"Of course I do," I said. "But rushing me into finding a job isn't going to suddenly make that happen."

Then, my father joined in still with his arms crossed. "Josefina, you need to chase your dreams while you're still young."

"What if I don't have any dreams?!" I said with an explosive tone of voice.

"What are you talking about?" my mother asked. "Of course you have dreams."

"I'm talking about what if I don't have any dreams?" I continued angrily and loudly. "What if being a dependent child is something I'm comfortable with right now? What if I don't know what I want to do with my life yet? Why are you forcing me to decide everything right now?!"

"How about we continue this inside so the neighbors don't have to hear all of this?" my mother suggested at a much lower volume level than I was speaking at.

"It's like telling a bear that it should be an elephant or something and expecting it to just fit the mold of whatever without figuring it out for itself," I continued my rant. "You can't just be, like, Josefina can be anything when clearly Josefina cannot be just anything. I can't be an elephant or a bear and I don't want to be forced into deciding now. I hate this day now! Both of you ruined it! The pancakes were just a delicious buffer. Aren't you proud of yourselves?"

After an abrupt landing, I stomped toward the screen door connecting the kitchen with the backyard and continued stomping until I sat in my chair at the table. Then, I sat with my arms crossed and refused to look at my parents as they sat on the opposite side of the table. I really was being a defiant child and was milking it for all it was worth. It was one of my go-to coping settings.

"Josefina, try to understand," my mother attempted being the calming voice in this battle.

"These are the facts: you graduated college in May, you turned 21 today, you're smart, capable. You also have no income, you're living at home, and you've never actually taken on the responsibility of career-type work," my father laid out the facts.

"Yeah, but dad, I majored in the Classics and Philosophy. I don't have any job skills. I can write a 20 page paper like a pro, but that's not exactly something I can brag about on a resume," I responded.

My father rebutted with, "Do you have a resume?"

"What do you mean?" I asked.

"Do you have a resume? Have you actually written a resume for yourself?" he answered with more questions like daggers.

"Well, sort of."

"What does 'sort of' mean?" he continued with the questions.

"It means I have written a resume for myself… sort of," I explained poorly. My dad just looked at me for a while and expected me to continue explaining this 'sort of' resume writing experience. "I was trying something out on my computer before I graduated. Maybe back in March. I Googled how to write a resume and tried to write my own. All I got was my contact information and education. That's as far as I got. I had no relevant experience to write down. Nothing I've ever done would be useful in an interview situation. So I left it blank. That's my 'sort of' resume story."

My dad looked at me in a puzzled way. My mother also looked quite confused.

"So you don't have a complete resume," my father said with disappointment.

I shook my head to clarify.

"When were you going to tell us that you needed help with this?" my mother chimed in in her usual concerned tone.

"I don't know. I was hoping it wouldn't be a big deal. I should have asked for help from school or you or something. I know. I know. I know I'm way behind on the job search and it's really my fault for not being proactive enough. I didn't really try looking. I was so caught up in final papers and exams that I didn't really make finding a job a priority. I don't need to hear a lecture about it," I said, looking down almost shamefully as a result of realizing my stupidity in this situation.

"Okay, Josefina," my mom said. She came around the table and gave me a hug. Then, out of nowhere, she grabbed the newspaper and pen from the table. She carefully placed the newspaper on the table, opened to the classifieds section, and pushed a pen in front of me. "Now is a perfect time to start looking for a job."

She started walking away and just as she escalated up the stairs, she called out, "It's only the beginning!" My dad followed her out of the kitchen.

I stared at the newspaper for a few minutes in a, *what are you looking at* kind of way. That soon changed to an, *I will conquer you* glare. That was the beginning.

CHAPTER TWO

"It is the mark of an educated mind to be able to entertain a thought without accepting it." –Aristotle

After a long time of glaring at *The New York Times* classifieds section, the staring contest grew old. I didn't see any listing for anything I was remotely interested in or had any qualifications for. There were listings for architects, a deli manager, software engineers, and the ever-elusive consultant job. I never really could decipher the actual essence of what a person did for a living when they would say, "I'm a consultant." Whatever that means. People always get all wacky when a consultant enters the room at a cocktail party. All t he hubbub never seemed to impress me. Honestly, you could do anything as a consultant. You could build a career on just saying you're a consultant and describing your work as, "Oh, I do a number of different things. I work with various companies and help them with their businesses. It's really rewarding." What exactly about having this mysterious, suspicious job is rewarding? It could just be the fact that you can get away with saying you're a consultant, when really you could be an out-of-work consultant who's just trying to save face. It's all a mirage. It's a job mirage, if you will. *That* would be my career path. That was my ticket. All I needed was to concoct some career that appeared like I was doing things and making money at it. I figured I could be consultant. It was the perfect career for me. Nondescript, vague, elitist, and in-demand – that was where I needed to go in life. As a consultant, I would have all the options in the world. I could choose which field I would be a consultant in. It's like being an expert. I went to Princeton University and studied the Classics and Philosophy. I could be an expert. Did it matter that there was basically no demand for a consultant in the Classics outside The History Channel? Nope. I could be a consultant if I wanted to be one. And it even had a job listing in the newspaper – sort of.

"Look, dad!" I called up the stairs in my childhood house in a way that sounded like Santa Claus had shown up for Christmas in June, or my birthday, which would have been even more awesome than Christmas in June. "I found a job!"

My dad descended on the stairs, walked through the kitchen and into the dining room, where he saw I had newspapers strewn about the room. It looked like I had been violently and unnecessarily looking through every inch of the Sunday *Times* to the point where it reached complete and utter chaos.

He sat down in a chair in the midst of the chaotic mess that surrounded him.

"What is it you want to show me?" he said as he put on his reading glasses.

Then, I pulled out a sheet of newsprint from the top of the pile and held it to my chest. "I may have found my calling. Hear me out. We all know that I haven't a clue of what I want to do with my life. We all know that if I had my way, I'd be 10 years old forever and play on my swing-set-jungle gym-apparatus and have tea parties and play with Barbie dolls. But I'm 21 now and society says I can't do that. I know that. So starting today – my 21st birthday – I'm going to make some big decisions about my life," I said with a surprising bout of confidence.

"Okay. So what is this decision you have made, Josefina?" my dad asked skeptically, readjusting his reading glasses. "I'm all ears."

I breathed in deep, absorbing stray particles of newspaper in my nostrils. And then I sneezed all over the newsprint page I was about to hand over to my father to read. It had a spot right the middle that had some booger goo. So I tried to save face by using another page to scrape the boogers off that prized page.

"*Salúd*," my father said in Spanish after I sneezed.

"Sorry," I apologized as I wiped my nose with my arm. "Back to this life decision thing."

"I'm ready. Fire away."

"Okay. So here's my life plan: I'm going to be a consultant," I said with the kind of enthusiasm a five year-old has when she's just made a bowl out of pink and purple Play-Doh.

"Uh huh," was all that my dad uttered.

"Yes! It's foolproof. People who are consultants or say they're consultants can work or pretend to work in any kind of field of expertise. I figure I could be an expert on the Classics or Philosophy since I don't really have expertise or qualifications for much else. I could go to cocktail parties and rub elbows with some people, get on some scholarly boards, and talk about Socrates and Epicurus or something like that." I handed him the snotty newsprint and said, "See?"

My father then paused for a moment considering my pitch. By the way he laughed, he didn't see it all the way I did. It wasn't like a hyena or a monkey laugh or something loud and wild. It was contained like a hearty chuckle with a dash of watching an Adam Sandler movie kind of laughter.

"Josefina," he said seriously after his bout of laughter. "I don't know if this is right, if you understand that the point of this is not for you to mold your career into something concrete now. Now is the time for you to explore your options. See what you like in a working environment. At this stage, your mother and I aren't expecting you to figure it all out in 10 minutes. That's not realistic. You also need to be realistic about this."

Tears were welling up behind my eyes, but I refused to look weak. All I wanted was to do something fun with my life that I could be proud of and preferably make a lot of money at. The problem was that I had stupidly not done any internships when I was at Princeton, so I had no work experience to speak of.

"Maybe do a little soul searching, eh?" my dad suggested.

I nodded as he took off for his home office to play computer chess and left me there stranded in a sea of newspapers with no signs of my future.

After sitting in the mess of a dining room and feeling sorry for myself for a half hour, I realized that no matter how upset my parents knew I was, sulking and acting like a spoiled child wasn't going to get me any attention this time. I was an adult and I needed to at least act like I wanted to be treated like one. So I made the newspapers into a chaotic jumble on the table and ran upstairs to my room to turn my job search into a Google search.

It was clear that being a consultant right out of college wasn't going to be a viable career option for me. Therefore, I decided to search online for the perfect career for me. One professor at Princeton actually told the class that we should make Google our best friend. So I made a friendly visit to my dear old pal to see what the Internet had in store for my future. It was like my Magic 8-Ball. I started by looking up job search websites. I found one that looked promising. It claimed that it could find a career match for me just by taking a survey. I tried to answer the questions honestly, but when I reached certain probing topics in the quiz, I felt inclined to answer with the more idealistic response. There were other questions that begged a specific response, but most of the answer choices seemed rather similar.

For example:
Of the following, how would you prefer others perceive you in a work environment?
    a. Hard-working.
    b. Taskmaster.
    c. Enthusiastic.
    d. Friendly.
    e. Trustworthy.
    f. Responsible.
    g. Lazy.
    h. Other.

In this situation, I certainly couldn't click on "Lazy" because being lazy just wasn't part of my work ethic. I could definitely be considered "Trustworthy." I've kept my best friend, Bethany's secrets for years. That takes a lot of trust. And being "Hard-working" or a "Taskmaster" were qualities that Princeton had drilled into my head considering, well, you know, it's an Ivy League university. "Friendly" and "Enthusiastic" were conditional. If I get a good feeling about a person, of course I'll be friendly. I can fake a smile like no other. And I'm always enthusiastic – as long as I like what I'm supposed to be enthusiastic about. "Responsible" was up to interpretation. I lost my guinea pig when I was six years old in the backyard. It ran away. I remember being completely afraid of it for some reason, so I appropriately named this rather fat, furry, little thing Monster. On the other hand, I always handed in homework on time. This question created some serious issues for me. I really wasn't sure which was the best answer to find a job I could live with doing day in and day out. So I picked the ominous "Other" option.

First of all, this quiz took far too long to complete. I probably spent nearly two hours contemplating my responses and reading the questions over 40 times each. There were only 10 questions in this survey. Second, I wasn't really sure that this quiz was legit. And third, the final outcome and the quiz's choice for my future career said I would be great as a delivery service employee. It recommended that I drive a truck and deliver packages to people. It even went as far as suggesting I aspire to be a manager of sorts in this field. Now, I don't have anything against the delivery industry or people who work in it, but really? That was what this quiz took from my "Other" answer? I just didn't see how this could be at all an accurate assessment of my future career. Either way, applying to a job at the Post Office was going to be at the very bottom of my list.

So I figured maybe career quizzes weren't the best option for my search. The problem was that I really had no idea what I wanted to do with my life. Naturally, I made a list. In true Josefina fashion, I took out a pink pad of paper and a sparkly pen and created a ledger of ideas for my future career. The list started out a bit over the top. I had written down some job prospects like talk show host, movie actress, and celebrity. As far as I was concerned, these were all viable options to start the brainstorming process. Celebrity was my favorite, of course. You could be a celebrity for doing anything – or doing nothing. Then, I started thinking about more seemingly realistic options. I jotted down psychologist, interior decorator, and professional blogger. My background in philosophy might be useful with a career as a psychologist but that would require me going to graduate school. I figured I could use my creativity to be an interior decorator. And blogging for money just sounded like a lot of fun. However, what exactly I would blog about was an enigma.

While I was considering these possible options for my future, Bethany called me.

"Hey, Josie! Happy birthday to you. Happy birthday to you. Happy birthday Josefina! Happy birthday to you!" Bethany greeted me on the phone with a song.

"Thanks, Bethany."

"What are you up to on this beautiful June day?"

"Well, now that you ask, I'm looking for a job, a career, and/or a future. I'm trying not to be too picky, but honestly, I haven't the slightest idea where to start," I replied honestly.

"I see," she said quizzically.

"If you want to help, I'd love to hear your two cents on what I should do with my life."

"So on your 21st birthday, you're celebrating by looking for a job?"

"Yes. That's exactly right. If I find a job or career or something to make money today, that will be my birthday present to me," I said. "Right now on my list I have psychologist, interior decorator, blogger, or my absolute favorite, celebrity."

"You're definitely planting your future the sensible way. Look, Josie, you know we've been friends for a while now…"

"Yeah. Since Freshman year at Princeton."

"Exactly. As your best friend of four years, I'm going to be honest with you," Bethany said in complete seriousness.

"Okay. I'm ready for this honesty."

14

"Well, if you're asking for my opinion, I think you need to brainstorm things you like, things you're good at, things you enjoy doing. Ask your parents for ideas. They might come up with something you never even thought of."

I didn't think this was the most far-fetched idea she ever had so I figured it was a plan of action I could live with.

Bethany continued, "Then, when you have an idea of what kind of things interest you that could be translated into a career or job or whatever, then think of where you need to be in order to make that happen."

"So relocation?" I asked.

"Yes," Bethany replied.

"Uh huh."

"You didn't think you would live with your parents all your life, right? You already lived with them your whole life and through four years of college."

"Yeah, well, I know that. I mean, I just, I didn't think this would all happen so fast."

Then, Bethany said something that really struck me. She said, "Welcome to adulthood, where everything happens faster than you want it to."

While her advice was well-intentioned, I couldn't help but feel pressured. This whole new debacle in my life felt like a pressure cooker and I had a feeling my parents were just waiting for me to leave and move out on my own. The problem was that I was so dead-set against certain kinds of jobs that there was no way I would dare consider them again.

"Anyway, what are you *really* doing for your birthday?"

———

I struggled for a couple of hours sitting in my room as my uncertain and confusing future loomed ahead. I was completely lost. I really didn't want to think about how I was going to have a really hard time finding a job. I didn't want to think about the pressure I was feeling from my parents. Everything about this was completely off. So I went where I knew everything always made sense: my swing-set-jungle-gym-apparatus.

It was already dark. I had told Bethany I decided not to go out on the night of my birthday, but that we should set a rain date. My mind was too preoccupied to go out. My swing set was right outside in the backyard, so I walked with bare feet onto the patio and felt the blades of grass from the lawn between my toes. Then, I sat on the seat of my swing set and immediately took off. I wanted to swing into space. That would have made me so happy, but I was smart enough to know that wasn't really going to happen. Still, I closed my eyes and imagined swinging toward the moon. It was always a childhood fantasy of mine that I would be able to go to the moon. I could float around in zero gravity and hang out with all the stars. I even entertained the thought of becoming an astronaut at one point, but as I grew older, I knew that wouldn't be a possibility for me. I could fantasize about it all I wanted, but I knew I would freak out sitting in a spacecraft that was taking off into the stratosphere. No one can hear you scream out there. Somehow, I felt like no one could hear me screaming for help with this job search. Maybe I was in a weird Earth-like version of space. I still had my eyes closed and I knew I was gaining momentum and height on the swing. This was the only place I could really think clearly. If I moved somewhere else for a job, I wouldn't have access to my swing-set-jungle-gym-apparatus whenever I wanted or needed it. I would miss that small morsel of freedom, but I knew I had to move on. This chapter of my life was coming to a close and a new one was bound to start. So long as I found a job.

CHAPTER THREE

"The most useful piece of learning for the uses of life
is to unlearn what is untrue." – Antisthenes

Bethany called me the next week to tell me she had a day off of work and desperately wanted to hang out with me. So of course, I cleared my already empty schedule.

When she arrived at my house, I was startled at the big, lingering hug that Bethany gave me.

"I feel like I haven't seen you since graduation," Bethany said.

"Yeah. That's probably because we haven't actually seen each other since graduation," I responded.

"Are you mad at me or something?" she asked. I hesitated on an answer to her question.

The shock on her face from the mere thought that I could be mad at her looked as if I had slapped her with a scary stick. I had to laugh. It was too easy.

"And now you're laughing?" she said in a very stern tone. I was doubled over laughing at this point. "Seriously, Josefina? What are you laughing at? All I asked was if you were mad at me." She started getting angry. That's when I knew to stop.

After an abrupt end to my laughing, I apologized and said, "But you should have seen your face, Bethany!"

"What do you mean?"

"If only I had a mirror to show you!" The laughing started up again.

Thoroughly annoyed at this point, Bethany played a clever card and said, "Take a picture. It'll last longer."

"Touché."

"I haven't lost my touch," she said proudly.

"I'll be the test of that! Last one to the swing-set-jungle-gym-apparatus is a rotten egg!" I yelled as I took off toward the screen door in the kitchen and into the backyard.

"Always a child," Bethany said to herself as she kicked off her flip-flops and ran outside to be the rotten egg.

Bethany and I had been best friends since freshman year at Princeton. We were in the same orientation group. Somehow the Puerto Rican and the girl with four different crayon colors in her naturally red hair clicked while everyone else was "bonding" and playing basketball in the gym. I saw Bethany Jenkins looking lonely in the bleachers and since I was pretty outgoing, I said, "Hey." She said, "Hey." We were inseparable on campus. She had my back and I had hers.

There was this one time we were out at an off-campus party. They had a keg of beer, jungle juice, and some Red Bull and vodka drinks set up at on the kitchen counter. I remember just picking up a red plastic cup full of some nondescript, horrible tasting beer and Bethany grabbed the vodka bottle and started pouring. I thought that would be the worst of it. Nope. I was wrong. Then, she grabbed a Red Bull can, cracked it open and poured as much as she could in this red plastic cup. She drank whatever was left over from the can separately from her highly-caffeinated concoction. Now this may not seem like such an out of the ordinary situation to be in: two college students enjoying themselves at a college party – no big deal. We've seen it in movies a million times. This was different. You see, earlier that week, Bethany failed a physics exam. When I said she failed, that meant she got a B. The next day, she got in a fight with her then-boyfriend, Greg, because she said he called her too much and she couldn't get serious with a needy guy. And then, to top it all off, she lost her precious agenda planner. That was a rough week for Bethany.

We walked up the stairs of this party house and took a seat near the landing where the stairs change direction. Bethany had been drinking that Red Bull and vodka beverage steadily to the point that she almost had an empty cup. She's not a hard drinker. At all. I knew she was going to lose it within the hour. I tried to get her out of the party, but she wanted none of that suggestion. Eventually, I was able to coerce her outside to the backyard. They had a swing set. I was not sure why. Like, what would a house-full of young, barely-adult dudes want with a swing set? I wasn't in the mood to figure it out. That crappy beer was clouding my sharp logic. Anyway, Bethany was on her third cup-full. We claimed seats on the swing set and as I sipped on that watery beer, Beth was drinking gulps of this hyperactive junk. It was as if her boyfriend had dumped her with a Post-it that was not only a Post-it, but it was the wrong color Post-it for the occasion. That didn't happen, so I was convinced that she was in crazy-mode.

"Red Bull tastes like gummy bears," Bethany called to me over the loud party music, even outdoors.

"What are you talking about?" I asked, really confused about what had happened to my extremely intelligent best friend.

"Red Bull tastes like gummy bears! You know, Josie, like gummy bears. Yummm!" she said and took a swig from her red plastic cup.

She had definitely lost it. After that, she started laughing like a crazed hyena that had too much canned caffeine and cheap alcohol. It was by far the weirdest thing I had ever seen her do. I just wanted to get her out of that party or slap her or something. She needed to get back to reality, but I knew that wasn't going to happen with the high she was getting from all of the Red Bull in her system. That stuff gave her wings all right.

Getting her back home was a struggle. We had to find a designated driver to drive us to her dorm, which is where I stayed that night. I finally got Bethany to sit on the couch in the living room while I found Drew, the sober driver. When I went back to get Bethany because we were leaving, she was laughing and laughing and laughing as if someone had given her laughing gas. This incredibly infectious laugh had spread to everyone else in the living room. This one guy, I think his name was Marcus, screamed/laughed in my face and said, "Your friend is the fucking shit, man!" I'm still not sure why he had to scream that in my face with his gross beer/jungle juice breath. So. Bad. Then, a song played on the stereo. Of course, it had one of those infectious and repetitive beats that easily installed itself in everyone's heads.

"Oh my God!" Bethany exclaimed. "I freaking love this song!"

Next thing I knew, she was up from the couch dancing with gross-breath Marcus singing along with the song.

"Ooh! Ooh! La La La!" the living room crowd joined in the drunken madness.

"All right, Bethany. We're going," I said as I grabbed her arm and started pulling her toward the door.

She answered, "But Josie, don't you wanna dance like a gummy bear?"

Then, she started to dance as though she were a gummy bear. It was a scary sight.

Finally, centimeter-by-centimeter, I got her to the car. Drew was really no help in the matter except for the fact that he was our ride back to sobriety. Now, when we reached the stoop of Bethany's dorm building, I thought it would all be over. Nope. I was wrong. I usually am in these situations. Bethany started dancing to imaginary music. I was really wondering what was in that Red Bull and vodka because damn, that stuff was strong. Then, she started singing "Ooh! Ooh! La La La!" in a very loud, out of tune voice.

"Come on, Josie! Sing with me!"

And so reluctantly, I did. I kept wondering why that watery beer I had earlier hadn't affected my inhibitions yet, but I just tried to play along. We sang the hell out of that song. In fact, if I never hear it again, that would be okay. I'm sure that would be okay with Drew, too, considering he endured Bethany's off-key and out of tune singing the whole car ride back to campus.

This was the Bethany I had never seen before. But here's the true testament to our friendship. We actually got back to the steps in front of Bethany's dorm. She was still dancing. When she was done dancing (or attempting to dance) she stood really, really still. I mean, really still, like Medusa turned her to stone or something. Then, she vomited on my feet. Yep. That's right. She threw up on my feet. Luckily, I was wearing flip-flops so my shoes didn't get ruined, but it was so disgusting I can't even accurately express it. That's friendship for you. Vomit on your best friend's feet and shoes, and you continue a friendship. That love runs deep. Really deep. Obviously.

Good thing Bethany grew out of that wild stage of her life, but I would still get phone calls at 11:37 PM from her crying about some missing spoon or something. That part never threw me for a loop. As her best friend, I was obligated to put up with her silliness – well, maybe not all the silliness, but at least some or most of it. And of course, she was obligated to put up with my flamboyant childishness.

———

"Have you heard from anyone since graduation?" Bethany asked me as we swung to our hearts' content.

"Not really. I haven't been keeping up."

"Oh," she said almost uncomfortably. "I've looked at some of the Facebook updates."

"Cool."

"I heard Ben and Shruti got engaged," she said attempting to engage me in gossip. "She posted a picture of the ring on her profile. It looks incredibly sparkly and big."

"That's nice. They've been dating since what – sophomore year? Good for them."

"You don't seem like you want to talk."

"Sorry. I've just been kind of preoccupied."

"Yeah, I know. Job hunting is a bitch."

"Is it? I haven't noticed," I said with more than an ounce of discouragement.

Then, Bethany remembered something very important. "Oh, Josie! I almost forgot! I told my dad that you're looking for a job. He said his company is looking for an intern and if you're interested, he would put in a good word for you."

21

"Doesn't your dad work as like vice president of some marketing place in New York or something?"

"Senior vice president."

"Okay. Well, what kind of internship is this? I don't have any experience with marketing. I don't know the first thing about marketing. Like, what is marketing all about? I have no idea. Could I really pull that off?"

"Josie, you are one of the smartest people I know," ever-optimistic Bethany said. "Do some research; I have no doubt that you would be able to pull it off."

"Uh huh. I'm not qualified for anything in the world outside of *The Iliad and The Odyssey* or Jeremy Bentham's theory of Utilitarianism. How do I try to act like I know something that I honestly don't know?"

"It's an *internship*. You're not expected to know everything. Didn't you do an internship your last semester at college?"

"Um. No. I did not. That is why I'm stuck in this predicament."

"Oh. I could have sworn you worked at some place senior year…"

"Well, I didn't. And aren't internships unpaid?"

"This one is paid. It would help pay for expenses."

"What expenses?"

"Well, the internship is in New York City. That's where the office is. You would have to live in the city. You would be too far living here in the middle of nowhere in New Jersey."

"Oh. Okay. So I'm expected to move to New York City? I haven't been to the city since my sophomore year Art History class. That was a while ago. We went to the MAMA museum."

Bethany took her turn at bursting out in laughter. "You mean the MoMA? The *Museum of Modern Art?*"

I stopped my swing and shot her a stink eye look. "I don't see what's so funny."

"You really don't go to the city very often, do you?"

I looked away from her for a moment and made a defeated, embarrassed sigh. "Okay, Bethany. Ha. Ha. It's not that funny. So I messed up a vowel. Whatever."

"Whew! That was a good one, Josefina. The MAMA!" and the laughing started up again.

So I started swinging again. Up and up I went while Bethany was developing a pain in her side from laughing so hard. Eventually, she came up for air.

"I'm glad you could get a good laugh out of my lack of knowledge of New York City," I retaliated. "How am I supposed to do this? How am I going to just move to New York? Like, do I just pack my bags and say '*Adios*' to my life here? Do I find a roommate? How do I find a roommate? I've never had a roommate before! This is going to be a disaster, Bethany."

"You can't think like that. It's going to be okay. All you have to do is go in for an interview. It's just an interview. If you get the job – I mean internship. If you get the *internship*, then you can start thinking about all of this."

"But what if I do land this internship? And what if they say, 'When can you start?' I don't have anything else to do so what if I say 'Tomorrow' or something as a reflex? Ugh! What do I do?"

I paused to collect myself. Getting myself worked up about a simple possibility for my limitless and yet, completely empty future was not logical by any means. I didn't even have an interview yet. All I had was the promise a "good word" from a potentially influential contact. This was not a time to lose my head. Preparations were in order.

"Are you okay, Josie?" Bethany asked. "Maybe you should get off the swing –"

"No. I mean, yes, I'm fine. I mean, no, I will not get off the swing. This swing is the only thing that really makes any sense to me right now. It's the only constant in my life."

"Well, there's no change yet. Everything is still constant. You can still have the swing. It's all yours. Okay?"

"Okay," I said as I took in a deep breath.

"First thing's first, though. Where's your resume?"

"My resume?"

"Yeah. You'll need it for the interview. If you get one, smarty pants."

"Is it bad if I don't actually have a real resume?"

"I don't know. What's a *fake* resume look like?"

"It's not a *fake* resume, Bethany. It just doesn't exist really," I cringed as I said that. I knew what was coming next.

"You don't have a resume?! Josefina, how are you expecting to apply for jobs and get a job without a resume?"

Bethany stopped her swing, got up, and stood in front of me with her arms crossed. She reminded me of my disapproving mother. I knew she was disappointed similar to the way I was disappointed in my own lack of preparation for the real world. Four years of Philosophy classes and lectures about Homer and Aristotle had left me unemployed, unemployable, and severely unhappy with my life in its current state.

"You need to work on this, Josefina. I think you need to work on this now. You needed to work on this back in sophomore year. I can't believe you don't have a resume!"

"Okay. Okay. Okay. You can stop lecturing me. You're starting to sound like my mother. If this resume thing is such a big deal and you're having a coronary about it, can you at least help me with it?"

She let go of the stern mother façade and walked me through the process of writing a resume. It was long, long overdue. Bethany made it a point to remind me of this every five minutes. It was either, "How could you not have done this before?" or "Why didn't you do any internships?" or my favorite, "Do you even know where the career office is at school?" This process was also very time consuming. From deciding the organization, the font to use, and how exactly to word the experience I did have, it was a form of cruel and unusual punishment.

"So babysitting shows some responsible characteristics, I guess. Being secretary of the Philosophy club at Princeton is an impressive accomplishment, in a way. What exactly did you do with the Philosophy club?" Bethany inquired about my barely existent job credentials.

"Well, we read a lot and then discussed what we read," I answered to the best of my ability.

"So the Philosophy club was like a book club?" she asked with scrunched eyebrows.

"Oh! We also had parties celebrating stuff like Plato's birthday."

"When is Plato's birthday?"

"Well, we're not actually sure of the exact date; it's up for debate. But we think he was born sometime around 428 BCE so on April 28, we like to celebrate his birthday. It's also usually the end of midterms for the spring semester so there's another reason to throw a party."

"Right. Okay. So skills include event planning."

"Well, I don't know about event planning. I know about baking a few cupcakes from a box and putting up paper streamers and stuff. I'm no event planner, Bethany."

"Go with it. It's a positive quality. It looks good on the page. Learn to embellish what you've done or can do. Seriously. I really can't believe you never went to the career office."

Eventually, after much hemming and hawing, Bethany and I printed out the first copy of a resume that I could be proud of and not feel like I was lying between the lines. I was very proud to have an actual, presentable, finished resume that had my name on it and had the potential to land me a job – or in this particular case, an internship. Just when I was admiring this piece of paper that happened to carry the weight of my future on its hypothetical shoulders, Bethany's phone rang.

CHAPTER FOUR

"Character may almost be called the most effec-
tive means of persuasion." –Aristotle

So I got an interview. Apparently, I was actually deemed eligible-slash-qualified for this internship. It was my first job interview. Ever. And I was on the verge of freaking out. I kept wondering if I was ready for real adulthood. The responsibilities and expectations that went along with being an adult were just too much for me to handle. I was about to get a job. Well, I was about to interview for a job. A job in an industry I knew absolutely nothing about. The only thing I knew about advertising was that commercials would always interrupt pivotal moments in my favorite TV shows and movies. So annoying. Basically, I had never been more anxious about anything in my life. This was completely uncharted territory that I needed to discover for myself. I was becoming an adult. To some, especially my parents, it was about time.

The snag in the whole job plan was this little place called New York City. I was so afraid of traveling to the city on my own. No. I was absolutely terrified. I could barely navigate the Princeton University campus for my first two semesters. I even kept a campus map in my school bag through my senior year just in case I got lost. It wasn't that I didn't have a good sense of direction; I just tried to keep to familiar routes. Bethany said I would get used to the pace of New York and that it wasn't so bad. She said that if I was able to survive the torture that was

Professor Schnell's Microeconomics class in my junior year and finish with an A, New York would be a breeze. God, that class was a headache.

I attempted rifling through my closet to find a presentable outfit for a New York City interview day. Avoiding looking like a small town girl from New Jersey was key. I think my mom heard me screaming at my closet and stomping my feet on the floor and throwing shoe boxes around and basically just being a household disturbance.

"Josefina, are you all right in there?" my mother asked as she knocked on my bedroom door.

That was when I collapsed on my bed and out came the waterworks.

Stepping into my room with caution so as to not step on an emotional land mine, my mother looked around at my progress or rather, assessed the damage left behind by Tornado Josefina.

"*Ay, Dios.* Well, honestly, I kind of expected worse. You know, considering the temper tantrum and everything," she said.

At that point, my face was buried in a pillow on my bed. I was accustomed to causing a domestic scene in an attempt to attract attention to whatever predicament occupied my mind at the time.

"You could have just come downstairs and asked me for help – with whatever you're trying to accomplish here," she continued, picking up clothes strewn about and the pieces of my broken spirit.

I rose from the pillow and wiped some tears away from my eyes. "What am I supposed to do, mom? My interview is tomorrow!"

"I wish you would have told me you needed help with an interview outfit before it became eight o'clock at night," she began sifting through the clothes that were strewn about the room.

"I know, mom, but this all happened so fast. Bethany got the call from her dad's secretary and we worked on my resume and everything only two days ago. I've also been trying to memorize the subway route I have take to get there so I don't look like a tourist," I said in my effort to make a logical excuse as to why I still had no interview attire.

"Sweetie, you *are* a tourist in New York City," my mother mocked me. I was unenthused.

Then she had a deep sigh and took a seat in my desk chair. "Josefina, tell me this. Aside from typing out your resume and 'everything,'" she emphasized the nebulous 'everything' I had referenced, "have you prepared at all for the actual interview? This is your first job interview, right? Do you know what to expect?"

"Not really," I said. "I Googled some articles, but I'm just kind of lost on this. I don't know what to focus on and the later it gets, the more I panic."

"Ay, Josefina. Why don't you ask for help when you know you need it?"

"I don't know, mom," I snapped. "You always ask me that."

"It isn't an unwarranted question."

"Yeah, well time is running out here and I don't know what to wear."

"Wearing a professional-looking outfit is very important for an interview. I've been on a lot of interviews in my time, you know. But I also know that you could be the most fashionable person to walk through those doors and if you can't answer the questions they ask the right way, what you're wearing will mean nothing."

My mother was trying to impart some of her knowledge from being a professional, working-woman as an office organization consultant most of her life. I knew that. I also knew that I knew nothing. I had no competitive advantage here. I would have to ask my mother for help with something aside from doing my laundry.

After a deep sigh, I gave in. "Okay, mom. Teach me your ways. What do I need to do?"

She told me to clean up my room in true professional organizer fashion. After that task was complete, I joined my mother in kitchen and sat across from her at the kitchen table. She had begun writing things on the index cards piled next to her. As instructed, I placed a copy of my resume in front of me.

"Okay, Josefina. I'm going to ask you some questions that you'll probably hear at your interview tomorrow. Ready?"

"Sure," I said with an air of overconfidence. I kept thinking, *I got this*, although I was nervous about answering these questions.

"All right. May I see your resume please?"

I passed my resume across the table to her. My mother looked over the sparse document thoroughly.

"So, Josefina, tell me something about yourself."

And immediately, that *I got this* turned into a complete blank in my mind. Then, I remembered this was practice and it was okay to make mistakes. I made my best attempt at an acceptable response.

"Well, my name is Josefina Ruiz. I'm Puerto Rican. I'm from Bellcastle, New Jersey. Um, I graduated from Princeton University in May. And I majored in Philosophy and The Classics. I was the secretary of the Philosophy club. I babysit sometimes? Um, my hobbies include watching movies and reading." I paused and tried to remember if I left anything out. "Oh, and I know how to use computers. Not like I'm a computer genius, but um, I can do normal word processing." I took a deep breath. "Was that good enough?"

"Not even close," my mother said. She then looked at the clock on the microwave. "*Ay Dios Mio.* There is just not enough time."

We worked on my interviewing skills for two hours. It was a crash course. Apparently, I needed a lot of work. After interview practice, I went upstairs and confronted my small closet. Oh, yeah, it was minuscule, narrow, and shallow. Luckily, my dad had built shelves above and below the curtain rod so as to create more useable space out of my diminutive wardrobe. One time, before the shelves were installed and I was younger, I would hide in my closet with my Barbie dolls, marshmallows, and a flashlight to have a night time camp out. Eventually, I scattered those glow-in-the-dark stickers on the inside of the door so the dolls would have stars to look at. Those were good times. Life was so much simpler as a seven year-old. That was the only reason why I could actually fit in that closet. Why did we have to grow up and complicate our lives with job interviews and questions about ourselves anyway?

I woke up early the next morning. It was so early that I almost rolled out right out of bed and onto my floor when I reached for my alarm clock that kept incessantly beeping at me. My interview wasn't until 3 p.m. and I had a genius plan to wake up at 7 a.m., however, I couldn't sleep and I was also not in the right mind space. I had to take a train from the Bellcastle station at 12:06 p.m. that would get to New York Penn Station by 1:48 p.m. The length of this train ride was unsettling to me. I figured there had to be a mistake in the schedule, but it turned out that it really did take over an hour and a half to get from Bellcastle to New York City by train. That meant I had more time to sit and contemplate the pending interview I had to look forward to. As for the hour gap in time between my arrival and the interview, I assumed I would probably need the full hour to actually get to the office. I was not a savvy New Yorker or commuter. I was Josefina Ruiz from Bellcastle, New Jersey and I needed a job.

The coveted interview ensemble I chose was hanging on a hook over my closet door. I stepped out of bed and just stood and admired it. My mind was actually tossed up between thinking *I'm going to look good* and *This is about as good as it's gonna get.*

Somehow, I had to make a black skirt, one of my mother's purple button down blouses, and a pair of black heels that I hadn't worn since high school graduation look believable on my jeans and t-shirt, Converse sneaker-wearing body. I was used to looking like a typical college student – not like a professional, or at least a wannabe business professional. There really should have been a required course at Princeton with a curriculum on the basics of presentable interview attire. I guess I didn't go to that kind of school.

I got to the train station almost a half-hour early because I was afraid of missing the only train that would get me to New York City in time for my interview. Walking toward the ticket booth, I could see an older man on the other side of the glass. I asked for a ticket to New York City.

His quick response was, "One-way or round trip?"

Apparently, I looked confused.

"Are you planning on returning to Bellcastle?" he asked.

"Oh! Yes! But hopefully not forever," I answered. He had no idea what I was talking about, so he became the confused one in the conversation. Jedi mind tricks were always my favorite means of communicating with strangers. If only Master of Confusion was an actual degree.

After 30 minutes or so, the train arrived at the station. Luckily, the Bellcastle train station passenger waiting area was indoors and air conditioned. Waiting in the July heat would not have been good for my, "I'm employable," look. Plus, pit stains really aren't flattering when meeting people who could give you a way out of your parents' house. I was thankful for the air conditioning in the station and on the train.

When I got on the train, I searched for an empty seat. I wanted a window seat. I always got a window seat on airplanes so it was natural for me to set out to find a seat where I had a clear, unobstructed view out the window. Eventually, I found one. It was a two-seater and I tried to channel the train seat gods and beg them to let me sit alone. But these so-called train seat gods failed me and while I was engrossed in looking out the window, someone decided to sit next to me. I actually didn't notice until a few minutes later when I turned my head and discovered someone sitting next to me.

"Hi," the person sitting next to me said. It was a guy's voice. I didn't actually get a good look at him until I turned away from the window. To my surprise, this was not just a creepy guy sitting next to me and greeting me on a train. This was a very cute guy sitting next to me and greeting me on a train. This was a cute guy with green eyes and brown hair in a decent hair cut. This was a cute guy with possibilities.

"My name is Malcolm," he introduced himself in such a friendly way, however I was quite stunned at my luck and forgot to speak.

"This is where you tell me your name –" Malcolm suggested.

I unfroze, but somehow still managed to avoid his probe for my name.

"So, is this a thing? People introduce themselves on the train? Sorry, I've never really been on the train before. I don't really know the rules," I said in a nervous manner. "I'm new to the train system," I whispered loudly so that no one else could hear me. But I knew they could.

Malcolm smiled at me for a moment and said, "You're very pretty. You know that?"

Then, I started blushing and pulled my thick black hair around my right ear. "Thanks," I said shyly. "I'm Josefina."

"Nice to meet you, Josefina. I guess I can't ask if you come here often," he joked to get a smile out of me.

I asked, "Are you going to New York, too?"

"Yep. I actually work in the city. I'm on my way over there now."

"I'm on my way to a job interview."

"If you don't mind me asking, where are you interviewing?"

"Well, it's really an internship, but it's at Jarvis Advertising and Marketing. It's on West 24th Street. Honestly, I have no idea where that is," and on came the nervous laughter.

It turned out that Malcolm's job was located near my ultimate destination. We talked the whole train ride to New York City. It was like having a train buddy. And when we got off the train, Malcolm walked with me from Penn Station to where my interview was. This was sort of a bad idea, though, because I had no idea how I got there in the first place since we were laughing and telling stories the whole way there. He did call it "downtown," which based on the fact that I had memorized most of the subway map, should have made more geographic sense to me. He did give me his business card before leaving me, though. According to his card, Malcolm was a park manager at Madison Square Park, which I vaguely remembered from the map. He wrote his cell phone number on the card and said to call him when I finished my interview and maybe we could grab some coffee. Coffee was starting to sound like a good idea once he left for work. I still had a half-hour before my interview and had nowhere to go. So I went to a coffee shop and had some iced tea. It cost me $4.50, but it was too hot outside for anything not iced.

While I enjoyed my cold beverage, I knew I had to text Bethany about this amazing encounter with Malcolm. My text message to her consisted of:

Me: OMG OMG OMG I JUST MET A HOT GUY ON THE TRAIN!!!

I knew that would get her attention. And it did.

Bethany: OMG SO EXCITING! FROM JERSEY? HAS JOB? HAS NAME? HOW OLD? DETAILS!!
Me: YES! YES! MALCOLM DODSON. 25. SUPER CUTE!

This all-caps conversation went on until my interview at 3 p.m. I got a "Good luck" text from Bethany just as I walked in the building and headed toward the elevator. I was instructed to take the elevator up to the eighth floor. While riding the elevator, I practiced my confident smile, stood up straight, and smoothed out my hair. My fingers got stuck in a huge knot in my hair when I tried combing through. Luckily, I was able to free my hand from the thick section of hair that did not want to let go. The elevator doors opened and all I could think was, *This had better work.* I took a deep breath and stepped forward in my high heels that were on the brink of giving me debilitating blisters at that point in the day.

My wobbly and painful walk to the receptionist's desk was met with the face of a blonde-hair-blue-eyed-model-type-looking woman who sort of looked like Britney Spears. She was captivated by something on her computer screen. I leaned further over the raised desk hoping she would notice my presence. With a bright smile, she turned to me and said in a distinct Southern accent, "Well, hello there! Welcome to Jarvis Marketing and Advertising! How may I help you?" I was taken aback by her perkiness. I made it a challenge for myself to see if I could top her Southern hospitality-type greeting.

"Hi! My name is Josefina Ruiz. I have an appointment with Mr. Jenkins," I said with a Miss America smile to boot.

"All right then, Josefina. I'll let Mr. Jenkins know that you're here. Sit tight!" the receptionist said as she got up from her expensive, ergonomically enhanced chair.

I turned around and took a good look at the welcome area of the office. It looked a lot like what I thought an advertising agency office would be. There were posters up on the walls in fancy, expensive frames filled with what I assumed were ads from past campaigns that the agency had produced. I sat on one of the chocolate brown couches. These couches actually made me crave chocolate; they were so comfortable. I didn't want to get up. I was actually temped to take my shoes off. And then, of course, in perfect timing, the receptionist returned, motioning for me to follow her. So I did. I sort of pet the couch as I got up. I tried not to make it look weird. It probably did look weird though.

The receptionist showed me down a long walkway with a few surprise turns on the way to Mr. Jenkins' office. She knocked twice on his door and I could hear him say, "Come in."

"Hi, Josefina. It's nice to see you," Mr. Jenkins said warmly to me. Then he turned to the receptionist and said proudly, "Brittany, this is my daughter's best friend, Josefina. They went to Princeton together. She's interviewing for the internship position."

I declared myself as winning already for successfully identifying a Britney Spears look-alike in New York City with the same name (albeit different spelling). Among the millions of people who live in this city, I was able to find a true döppelganger for one of my favorite singers. This was my day. And this interview was going to go well. I could feel it in my bones. I had some good karma on my side.

Brittany acknowledged my apparent "in" with the boss-man with a big smile that I was starting to think was her go-to face for most things. "Well, then. I'll let you get on with your interview. Good luck!" she said, turned, and left me to fend for myself in this new world.

Mr. Jenkins invited me to sit down in one of the cozy chairs situated in front of his desk. Just as I started getting comfortable, he asked me one of the questions I had been dreading.

"Well, I know you went to Princeton and majored in Philosophy. Right?" he asked.

I nodded. He continued.

"Tell me something about yourself that I don't already know."

I gulped. Then, I took a deep breath. And then, I gulped again.

"Um," I started and almost winced for starting with "um." The truth was that I was wracking my brain for something interesting about myself that might seem relevant to this interview. Then, with a spark of genius, I started surprising myself, "the way I see it, sir, is that there are only a select few advertising slogans – they're called slogans, right?" Mr. Jenkins nodded his head and held out his hand urging me to continue. So I did. "So there are few advertising slogans that really can be considered iconic and surpass the confines of a specific time

34

and place. For example, Got Milk? *That* is a lasting campaign. I mean, people made T-shirts and coffee mugs about it! It made an impression. And everyone knows what it stands for and what it means. Now, I don't know a lot about advertising – yet – but that's what's important in advertising, right? It has to be like that song you can't get out of your head. Not in an obnoxious way, but in the way that people want to go and download the song immediately. They just gotta have it." And if that insight wasn't already surprising and impressive to Mr. Jenkins, what I said next was even more surprising and impressive to myself. "I know I haven't studied advertising or anything really business-y, but I'd like to do that, Mr. Jenkins. Or at least learn more about it. I studied Philosophy and that may sound completely boring and unrelated to advertising, but I think I have something different to bring to the table here. I want to help create the next can't-get-it-out-of-your-head campaign. I think I would be pretty good at it." And exhale. I had just given the speech of my life and I didn't even really prepare for it. It was almost like my midterms at Princeton.

Mr. Jenkins sat there, nodded a few times in a contemplative state, and said, "Josefina, that was quite an impressive insight."

"Thank you, sir," I said. "My mother says I have a very active imagination." He laughed at that.

After I answered a few more tough questions, I walked out of the Jarvis Advertising and Marketing offices feeling pretty confident. My weird and silly personality actually seemed to be well received. Whether I landed the position or not was one thing, but at least I knew I did the best I could do. I was also aware that that attitude wasn't going to solve my problem about finding a career job in something – anything – anything at all.

There was no way I could forget about Malcolm though. I was high up on this cloud and nothing was going to bring it down. Not even rain.

CHAPTER FIVE

"A great city is not to be confounded with
a populous one." – Aristotle

I never knew it before, but New York City gets really smelly when it rains. That lack of awareness may have been because for some reason, I had only been to the city maybe three times in my whole life – including this interview day. It was pathetic. I lived in such relatively close proximity to this glorified city. I have one thing to say about that: if New York is such a great city, why does it smell so much?

I had texted Malcolm after my interview from the building lobby so as to not get my ancient phone wet; it was pouring out. He said to meet him at the Madison Square Park entrance at the corner of 23rd Street and Broadway. I was not very pleased about walking in the torrential rainstorm that had started – especially because I had no idea where I was going. So I tried asking people on the sidewalk how to get to 23rd Street and Broadway from 24th Street and Sixth Avenue. This proved to be a difficult task. People were not so willing to stop and answer some lost girl's question while their once perfectly coiffed hair got soggy. I decided to take matters into my own hands and tried to find this street corner myself. Venturing into the shower-like rain was like an uphill battle. It was windy and sticky and gross. Considering I would usually love splashing in puddles and dancing in the rain (my mother always got annoyed when I did that), shielding myself from the weather was not typical for me. By the time I reached 23rd Street (I read the sign from a block away), I was already drenched. Figuring out which way would get me to Broadway was another challenge.

The forecast said nothing about rain. My mother's favorite news station always seemed to be wrong about the weather and I no longer subjected myself to listen to their inaccurate weather team to plan my day. My (mother's) button-down shirt that was a shade of vibrant purple now had large blotches of dark violet that were quickly populating the entire surface area. At least the wet parts of the shirt hid the pit-stains I attributed to both the interview and the summer heat. It was beginning to look like the blouse was all different blotchy shades. My hair was another story all together. I looked like I had just stepped out of the shower – while wearing all of my clothes. I considered pulling my long black locks into a ponytail to minimize the water damage, but upon attempting that feat, I realized that my hair had become a frizzy, stringy mess.

My natural indecisiveness was getting in the way of my journey to Malcolm. I felt bad thinking he was standing outside in the rain on the corner of 23rd Street and Broadway. Wherever that was. If he weren't that cute, I definitely wouldn't have made all of the effort drudging along in sheets of New York City rain for just anyone. My feet started making squishy sounds in my shoes. People started taking shelter under store awnings to wait out the storm. I must have looked like a complete idiot taking on the storm in what seemed like the right direction, but then again, what did I know? I probably walked up and down 23rd Street about six times. I would go one direction for a few steps and immediately think that was the wrong way. This repeated a few times. I could have just asked someone which way it was. These New Yorkers who were smart enough to step out of the rain for a while must have been watching me and thinking, "That girl doesn't come here very often, does she?" That wasn't really a question. They knew. It was obvious.

Finally, I tried asking someone standing under the awning to a store that apparently sold cookies for directions to Broadway and 23rd Street. I stepped under the awning just enough to catch what felt like a bucket full of runoff from the edge of the awning on my right shoulder. Clearly, this was not the rain I was used to.

"Honey, are you all right?" a (mostly dry) woman asked me as I got pummeled with disgusting New York City rainwater.

Not even thinking as I responded, I said, "Oh yeah. Rain happens. I'm already wet. What's a little more rain, right?" I literally brushed the water off my shoulder. Not figuratively. I could actually brush off the water that was forming a puddle on my soaked blouse.

"No, I meant, like, are you lost or something?" the same woman asked me in my exhausted state. She was wearing a dress with diagonal blue and green stripes. I really liked her dress. Those shades of aquamarine blue and emerald green were always my favorites. Most of all, it was a dry dress! I suddenly snapped out of dress-envy.

"Lost?" I was confused by her confusion. Obviously I was lost. But then I remembered what the whole intention was before I got crap water (I couldn't think of a more scholarly name for it) so rudely poured on me.

"Yeah. You seem lost. You've been walking up and down the block for, like, 10 minutes," the woman in the dress I wanted clarified.

"Oh. Well, yeah. I'm trying to get to 23rd Street and Broadway and I have no idea which direction it's in. And I don't want to walk too far and then have to walk back the other way when I don't get there after a while. And it's raining and hot out. And this crap water just keeps dripping on me. Rain shouldn't be this gross. I just need to get to Broadway," I rambled desperately.

Then she said, "Broadway? It's East from here."

My face could have had *¿Qué?* or What? written on my face at that point. East, West, North, South. It all meant nothing to me. I'm not Christopher Columbus. I wasn't trying to discover New York City in the name of Puerto Rico. I was just trying to get to Broadway.

She got the hint from my confused face. "That way," she directed with her arm extended her left, or East from here.

As I headed in the correct direction toward Broadway, my phone buzzed notifying me that I had an incoming phone call. I ducked under a store awning to answer the call. Do as the New Yorkers do. It was Malcolm.

"Hey, Josefina? It's Malcolm. You know, we met on the train today," he said apprehensively even though he was the one who called me.

"Oh, yeah. I think I remember you now," I said as a joke. He laughed. It worked. It was just another aspect of my brilliant mind. I figured if the advertising job doesn't work out, I could always be a stand up comic.

"I'm just calling because you texted me, like, 20 minutes ago saying you were on your way. Broadway isn't really that far –" Malcolm inquired with a concerned tone. "Just wanted to make sure you didn't get lost – or decide to bail. I'd completely understand with this crazy rain – "

"Me, lost? ¡*Imposible*! I think I'm getting close to Fifth Avenue. Am I close?" I asked him just as a taxi drove by and splashed through a huge crap water puddle on the road. This water splash traveled so far into the sidewalk that I wasn't safe even when standing under an awning far from the curb. A little bit of the water seeped into my shoes, which was really, really gross. And smelly.

I tried shielding my disgust over my garbage-filled shoes. I would need to disinfect my feet when I got home. The water was not helping with the blisters I already had either. I was pretty sure that I was going to get a nasty disease from that water.

Anyway, Malcolm said that I was close. And then he asked me, "Do you have an umbrella?"

"Well, I'm kinda really drenched right now so…" Just at that moment, a guy in a fancy suit walked by attempting to tame his umbrella, but the wind got the best of it. The umbrella basically ripped to shreds in a matter of seconds. I couldn't help but try to remember what I was still even doing here in this storm. It was like a hurricane. "Yeah, no umbrella."

"Okay, well you're really close. I'm sure this weather will pass soon," Malcolm assured me. "If you can help it, just watch out for the umbrella peddlers. They can be kind of a rip-off. It's a New York thing."

I headed back on my journey with a deep breath, crap water shoes, and no umbrella.

Then, I heard a loud voice coming from the corner ahead of me. Malcolm said that would be Fifth Avenue and that Broadway followed. He said that he would be at the entrance of the park with a green umbrella waiting for me. As I got closer, I heard what the man was saying: "Umbrella, umbrella, umbrella. Umbrella, umbrella, umbrella." This man kept repeating this chant as people walked by. It was evident that umbrellas weren't doing a whole lot of good in this particular storm. Meanwhile, he was keeping mostly dry in a dark blue poncho. Either way, he was going to sell some umbrellas. Malcolm had already warned me about this so I ventured on to Madison Square Park – not Madison Square Garden. Apparently, there was a difference.

When I finally reached Madison Square Park, Malcolm just kind of looked at me, smiled and hustled me under the umbrella like that was going to do a lot of good in drying me off. He took me to this hut-shed-house where he worked. We walked into the hut-shed-house and he handed me a towel. Like a towel would really help at that point. I was beyond towels. I needed that New York City summer heat back. Pronto. I thanked him for the towel anyway. He was being hospitable. All I kept thinking was, *This had better be worth it.*

"It's pretty bad out there, isn't it?" he asked almost rhetorically. We both knew the answer to that question.

He sat in a comfy leather chair and invited me to sit down in the comfy leather chair next to it. I placed the towel under my butt since I was soaked from top to bottom. I didn't want to get the chair too wet. Some dampness was inevitable at that point, though.

"This is one of my favorite places in the park," Malcolm said.

I looked around and aside from the comfy leather chairs, it was kind of small and dark. There were a few lamps bringing some light into the room, but honestly, it felt like we were camping in a cabin in the woods somewhere. Instead, Malcolm claimed the hut-shed-house in the middle of the park as his favorite place. And he was sharing it with me. My favorite place at my house was my swing-set-jungle-gym-apparatus and I only shared that with Bethany. Already, I could tell he liked me.

"It's… cozy," I responded awkwardly as I attempted stroking my hands through my hair. My fingers got stuck on a few knots.

"I bet you can't wait to just go home and feel clean and dry."

"Well…" I started to utter something.

"It's okay. If you want to go, it's okay. I'll walk you to Penn Station," Malcolm said.

"No, I'm fine here," I looked around the hut-shed-house another time. "Like I said, it's cozy in here. You've made this place very comfortable. These chairs aren't playing around. I'd like to stay – at least until I dry off a bit more. Plus, I look like someone who went to a water park in the wrong clothes right now."

He laughed at that, but it was true. My hair was a hot, dripping mess. I couldn't get a handle on it. If I put it in a ponytail, my hair would get all knotted and I would end up having to cut the elastic band out. If I let it stay loose, I was positive the stringy, grossness would only get worse. It was a lose-lose situation. I wouldn't consider myself a beauty queen at all. I mean, I wore jeans and a T-shirt or a sweater or a sweatshirt almost everyday I was at Princeton. And that was for four years. However, in this case, I felt like I had no real options except to look ugly with mascara smudged on my face, soaked clothes, crap water-filled shoes, and stringy hair, which smelled like wet garbage courtesy of New York City. Such is life.

CHAPTER SIX

"Learning is not child's play; we can-
not learn without pain." – Aristotle

After that fateful day in the big city, I had nothing to do but sit around on my butt back home and check my email incessantly waiting for a decision from Jarvis Advertising and Marketing. My mother was especially thrilled about it, not. She suggested I get out of the house for a while. That was my cue to go out to the backyard and sit on my swing-set-jungle-gym apparatus and text Malcolm. Malcolm and I texted each other a lot. We were getting along famously and he had quite a sense of humor. He barely knew me, but he knew how to make me laugh. I hadn't actually seen him since my interview in Manhattan and subsequent street shower, but we had kept in touch. The guy had seen me looking at my best and at my worst and still wanted to get to know me. Anyway you looked at it, he had serious boyfriend potential. I never had a boyfriend before so that judgment is based on what I saw in romantic comedies and from Bethany's love life. He also tried to keep my spirits up regarding whatever news was bound to come from J.A.M. – it was easier and faster texting an acronym than spelling out "Jarvis Advertising and Marketing."

The anticipation of waiting to hear back about the internship was really getting to me. All I wanted to do was go online and look up apartments, roommates, and living situations in New York City. But that seemed a little too presumptuous and I needed all the good karma I could get. So I stopped doing that. I tried reading through old philosophy textbooks from college to pass the time. I thought that revisiting what I had learned before would help propel me into a new world of knowledge. I was hoping Aristotle had some wise words to share with me. I even re-read Homer's *The Odyssey* just for fun. Reading the story of Odysseus's epic journey to get home got some thoughts turning in my head. It was a story of making choices to make it to the place where he truly belonged. I could relate. In my story, however, figuring out where to find these "choices" was becoming fruitless and painful. I wasn't prepared for the decisions I had to make about my future. The clock was ticking and everyone I knew was saying different things to me about what to do next, what kind of career fields I could venture into, and the hot topic on my parents' mind: where I would live. It seemed that the people who brought me into this world just wanted me out of their house. Despite the fact that they would tell me countless times that I should take my time and do this right, I could sense their true motivation. After raising a child for 21 years and paying for an expensive Ivy League education, they wanted a little freedom. I could understand that. Yeah. Sure. That made sense except for the fact that I still had no career prospects and next to no real job training aside from the ability to write the hell out of a 20-page research paper. Basically, they were ready to send me out into the world without an exit plan. So much for sound parenting methods.

My inner monologue thoughts were exhausting. So I put down *The Odyssey* for a spell and decided to take a nap. I kept my phone nearby just in case I got a call from J.A.M. I didn't want to jinx it, but I certainly didn't want to miss the call. I made sure it was set on a ringtone.

In dreamland, I envisioned a clear sky in my direct view. A few scattered clouds floated into the picture, but mostly it was sunshiny and bright. Note: it was not like a report on The Weather Channel. I was sprawled out on a lush, green lawn and started making grass angels with my arms and legs. Then, I sat up and saw the world around me. It seemed familiar like I had been to this place before. There were trinkets from my childhood like the doll my *abuelo* gave me when we visited Puerto Rico when I was six. I named her Girl. I was such a creative child. Ironically, my Barbie Dream House with the deluxe crank up elevator and backyard pool attachment also existed in dreamland. My childhood dolls were calling for me to play with them. So I did. In my dreamland, I was, like, seven years old. It was such a simpler time. I could make up my own stories for my dolls and toys to live out and not be told that it wasn't realistic. After having a hunky-dory time catching up with Barbie, Ken, and Skipper, I noticed the holy grail of the playground. My swing-set-jungle-gym-apparatus made a guest appearance in my dream. Of course, seven year old me didn't walk, but rather took off running to the swings. As I ran toward the swings, the sky turned dark and it started raining. Soon, the ground beneath me was soggy and full of puddles – all the better for me to jump in. Splash. Splash. Splash. I felt the muddy water splatter on my tiny legs like a summer sprinkler. I sat on the swing set seat despite the accumulation of rainwater that bubbled on the surface. I was one with the swing. I was swinging back and forth in a violent, swift, rhythmic motion. No one could tell me it was childish or crazy for me to be on a swing in the rain because in my dreamland, I *was* a child! And maybe I was a little crazy, too. All the conflicting thoughts and opinions that had been controlling me washed away. I was alone and free. I was unstoppable on that swing set. The swing suddenly settled to a silent halt where my feet could reach the soft ground, but I rejected that feeling under my feet. I wanted to feel the cool, wet air sprinkle my face in mid-swing. It was just like my real life, only not at all. It was dreamland. Dreamland was what I wish my life could be. Just playgrounds and puddles. Swing sets and slides.

BEEP! BEEP! BEEP! BEEP! My phone rang and buzzed, violently disturbing my adventure in dreamland. I was so deep in the dream that I actually levitated off my bed when the loud, buzzy tone forced my eyes open and woke me up. I looked over to see who was responsible for the incoming call. It was a 212 number and knowing that was a New York area code, I knew it was from J.A.M. Slightly disoriented from the loud, alarming sound, I tried to smooth my hair and pick the sleep out of my eyes as if it mattered what I looked like when speaking

on the phone. *BEEP! BEEP! BEEP! BEEP!* My phone continued its irritating tirade on my nightstand. Before finally answering the phone, I tested out my post-nap voice. "Hello?" too sleepy. "Hello?" too raspy. "Hello?" too fake. I didn't want to sound like I had just woken up and seem to be some lazy, unemployed college grad. Just before the last few rings and buzzes, I sat up (with good posture) and answered the phone with a confident, "Hello."

"Hello. Is this Josefina Ruiz?" the woman on the other side inquired.

"Yes. Yes, it is." I answered with a self-assured attitude.

"This is Joan Smiley from Jarvis Advertising and Marketing," the woman introduced herself. "Sorry for the wait on our end. There were a lot of really fantastic and qualified applicants for our internship program. Mr. Jenkins was very impressed with your interview."

Did anyone call him by anything other than Mr. Jenkins?

"He said you were very unique. That is definitely a treasured quality in this field. Thinking outside of the box is very important. I can't emphasize that enough – especially to someone with as much promise I'm told you have."

Like a bloodhound, I could sense the disappointment oozing all over every word she uttered before she even said it.

"However," Joan Smiley said sans smile.

And there it was.

"Like I said, there was a large number of applicants for the internship program this year. Unfortunately, we're at capacity and we can't offer you the position at this moment."

Of course, at this point my eyes welled up with tears and my fake smile reserved solely for sounding perky on the phone had flipped upside down. I tried to fight back tears and that awful sound in your voice that immediately sends out a universal signal that you are upset and are beginning to cry.

The most I could muster up to say was, "Okay."

"I'm sorry to give you that news. I know it's disappointing. It's just a very competitive market and advertising is pretty cut-throat. Maybe with more experience in the industry, you'll make an even better applicant next year," Joan said apologetically.

"Uh huh," I said, sniffed my nose a little (away from the phone), and asked the question I needed to know the answer to. "Is there anything I could have done differently? Maybe I could make some improvements."

Joan responded, "Well, I didn't sit in on your interview, but from what I do know, you seemed confident, inventive, and well-prepared."

A-ha! I knew those flash cards on advertising I made from searching the Internet would help. I was the queen of cue cards in college.

"I think some more professional work experience would help you build a stronger profile," Joan Smiley encouraged me.

"Thank you. I appreciate that," I said genuinely and followed up with the million-dollar question, "But how does someone get experience without experience?"

She paused for a moment and tried to generate a good response. "I'm actually not sure how to answer that. I'll be honest with you; apply again. Persistence does go a long way in this business. This is a great agency to work at. You would learn a lot here. If only we had enough spots –"

"I understand. Thanks again. I guess I'll have to just try and do something else for now."

"Please don't let this discourage you. Best of luck, Josefina," Joan Smiley ended the conversation.

I leaned back into the headboard of my bed for a minute and allowed myself to shed some tears of disappointment. After wiping away those salty streams flowing down my face, a feeling of *Crap. What the hell do I do now?* washed over me. I was back at square one with no square two to jump to. There was no Plan B or C or even W for that matter. I was doomed to be an Ivy League graduate who would work as the neighborhood dog-walker as a full-time job. My skills, qualifications, and connections were stretching pretty thin. A wave of anger followed. I stared at my phone for a while as if it was the dagger that was digging and twisting into my back. The impulse to throw my phone at the wall seemed like a good idea at the time, but I decided to chuck my stuffed penguin across the room instead. I figured Pengie could bounce back faster than a busted cell phone. I placed my phone beside me on my bed giving it the evil eye for being the bearer of bad news and the killer of my favorite dreamland ever. After punishing my phone with the evil eye for about 10 minutes, it turned into the stink-eye. Essentially, one of my eyes was almost bulging out of my head. I looked like a crazy person staring at a cell phone on a powder blue beaded princess comforter. And then, of course, on cue, my phone rang with its incredibly loud buzz and piercing beep tone, I yelled at it, read the message from my mother saying she was on her way home from work, and leaned back against my headboard.

"I really need to change that ring tone," I said to myself.

Next step was telling my mother and father the disappointing news of the day. Crap.

Before I could face my parents, I decided to take a ride to the Bellcastle Public Library. Books were always my solace. Now, I needed help. I needed to know what to do. I needed to be inspired. So off to the library I went.

I arrived, opened the heavy, antique-looking entry door, and took in the scent of the library. The sweet smell of stories was so inviting. Every shelf that surrounded me contained knowledge that I knew would lead me to the future my fate had intended for me. I walked the perimeter of the store slowly in order to absorb the titles and authors etched on the spines of the books that lined the walls. The shelves actually stood from the floor to the high ceiling. A rolling ladder allowed customers to see the selection on the top rows. I always thought the rolling ladder was really cool. When I was a kid, my mother would yell at me for trying to climb the ladder and propel myself across the wall. I would escape her hold and say I was going to look at the children's section. Engrossed in whatever book she was looking at, she would somehow lose track of the only little Puerto Rican girl in all of Bellcastle. So of course, panic-stricken, my mother would rush over to the children's section with no luck of finding me. Then, she would look under every table and check every aisle. Eventually, she realized she couldn't let me go anywhere without her so long as there was a rolling ladder on a track spanning three full bookshelves. One time, she even had a librarian at the circulation desk page me.

"Would Josefina Susana Ruiz please come to the circulation desk? Your mother is looking for you."

I was never easy to hold on to. Having a very active imagination made it difficult for my parents to rein me in – especially as a child. I had definitely gotten worse over the years. Still, libraries have always been kind of like intellectual sanctuaries for me. The library at Princeton was one of my favorites. That library has 70 miles of bookshelves! The size and scale of that library were just incredible. I would study in there and discover reading material; I was known to spend hours on end just exploring.

Looking through the aisles of the public library in Bellcastle, I came across a section of business and career books. I knew this was a subject I needed to educate myself about more. Book titles ranged from *Writing the Most Effective Cover Letters, Business 101 for Dummies*, and my personal favorite, *So You're Looking for a Job: 200 Ways to Get Hired*. That one seemed most relevant to me, but I still doubted there were actually 200 different ways to get hired, as the title boasted. But then, I was quite inexperienced in that area so my opinion on the topic was completely erroneous. Regardless, I pulled out that last book along with a few others and carried the heavy pile to a big, comfy chair by one of the large windows. I set the pile of books down beside the chair I chose to plant myself in. First, I pulled the top book in my stack. *Choosing the Right Career for You* was all about connecting personal interests with job skills and related careers. My first thought was that I wished I thought to do this research earlier. Of course, I had done research via the Internet, but I was also a little more old-fashioned about research. I must have had a lapse in sanity for not going to the library or at least a bookstore first when the whole "You need to find a job, Josefina" crap started happening. I flipped through the book to see if it could tell me something I didn't already know. Turns out, it couldn't. I figured that if I was able to make some sort of positive impression at an advertising agency in New York City, even if I didn't land the position, it was still a worthwhile impression. Therefore, my gut told me to stay on the same path and eventually it just might pay off. Whether that was what I was truly meant to do with my life was another story, but for now, advertising would do.

I thumbed through the pages of the other 17 books I had picked out. I wasn't playing around when I said I needed help. Nothing really struck a chord with me. Most of the books all said the same exact thing or the book seemed out of date or the book was not even relevant to solving my problem. I thought that I was done with all of the books in the ginormous stack of books beside the ginormous chair I was sitting in. I sighed at the new stack I had created full of discarded books from the original pile. It was disappointing how out of almost 20 relevant books, none of them seemed to contain information that I could really take and find beneficial in the present and near future. I was at a crossroads in which every direction I could take would lead to either another few roadblocks or the end of the trail. I couldn't win the way I was going. Knowing that fact made me even more frustrated with my situation.

Then, my phone buzzed in my bag with its incredibly distinct and loud vibration setting. I was in a library. Loud noises are not exactly welcome. I swear the sound just carried and reverberated throughout the entire library. Suddenly, I could feel the eyes of everyone there fixated on me. That included the 75 year-old woman intently reading her romance novels in the quiet privacy of the corner behind the historical books section, the 30-something year-old dude looking through every single sports magazine like it was his job, the mother of two (both still in a stroller) who was finishing borrowing picture books for her children at the circulation desk. While it was better than playing the "PENIS" game in the middle of the main reading area, having a phone ring in the library was the equivalent of me walking in the doors with a blaring boom box on my shoulder '90s style. It was a disturbance regardless of what the disturbance actually was. So, I promptly and quietly returned the books to their Dewey Decimal System placements on the shelves of the business and career section, and then I left.

When I got outside, I was hit with a wall of 97-degree heat. It was hot and humid. That library air conditioning was looking pretty desirable, despite my slightly embarrassing phone blunder. Then I remembered to check my phone to see who had tried to reach me.

MALCOLM: Hey. Hope you're not melting today. Lol.

How sweet! Malcolm was thinking of me. And he read my mind! It was crazy that I liked him so much since I had only spent that one day with him in New York. We had some sort of connection. There was something uncanny about how he just plopped himself on the seat next to mine on the train. He had a confidence I had never seen in a guy before. I was used to the polar opposites of the ultimate nerd who loved playing Dungeons and Dragons with fellow nerds and the popular hot jock who just wanted to play beer pong in between classes. I had met both of those fine examples. Finding someone worth my time who managed to be smart, funny, attractive, available, and actually a dude (not necessarily in that order) was a task I almost refused to engage in when I was in college. Of course, I looked around. I was open to meeting a guy during all four years at Princeton. Meeting the right guy was a different challenge. Maybe I just had to wait for him to come along. Maybe I had to wait for Malcolm. Did I really have to wait so long?! I'm a huge believer in the idea that everything happens for a reason, but when that "everything" takes 21 years to happen, it makes me question the personal philosophies we live by. I had never been on a real "date" before. This was a running record considering I *still* hadn't experienced a proper date or a proper kiss in my 21 years of life. Hoping that Malcolm wasn't just playing with my feelings and mind, in pure scholar mode, I decided to ask him about his intentions with me.

ME: What are your intentions with me?

Yep. I asked it just like that.

MALCOLM: What do you mean?
ME: Your intentions. With me. Intentions.

I then realized maybe I wasn't being as clear as possible. Remember: he's a dude. No matter how smart he may be, he could potentially not understand a word I was texting.

ME: Do you want to date me? Or be my friend?
MALCOLM: Both.

It was the simplest, most mature response I had even received via text message. The fact that it came from a guy was even more exciting. I nearly started crying right then and there in the sweltering library parking lot. I almost did. Instead, I ran to the car to turn on the A/C. And of course, the air that came through the car vents in my 13 year-old Toyota Corolla actually felt like a person blowing air on me. As if that would make me feel cooler. Clearly, my car was not conditioned for this New Jersey summer heat wave. This was the car that had gotten me to and from Princeton for four years. And suddenly, the air conditioning didn't want to work properly. I was melting, just as Malcolm had joked. Well, I was not joking at that point. I knew I had to get home and into my cool, air conditioned house. So I started the car and drove home. I left the windows open to generate some breeze while I was driving. However, that seemed to backfire as my previously sleek, dark hair had now been thoroughly blown around my head so it looked like I was a drunken sailor working on a ship in the humid, salty ocean air. Surprisingly, the piece of crap didn't overheat or leave me stranded on the road somewhere. I guess we have to count our blessings.

The journey from my car door, across the driveway, through the lawn, and up the front steps to my house felt like I was walking through the Serengeti. I was only wearing a tank top, shorts, and flip-flops and yet everything was sticking to me. I would pull my shirt away from my back to create some air circulation, but then it would return to its new occupation of sticking to my back. It was disgusting. It was unbearable. It was torturous. But most of all, it was sticky. I was sweating from places I didn't know could sweat. With the front door almost open, an ice-cold strawberry margarita appeared in my mind and I had one of those mirage moments like from those movies where the guy had been venturing through the desert for days without water and started seeing little oasis spots where there were none. Yeah. I was like that guy for a minute.

I opened the door after dropping my keys on the steps about four times. One would wonder if I actually had a margarita or two before opening the door because immediately upon opening it, I almost fell into the doorway just to touch the cold hardwood floors in our foyer. Honestly, I was too exasperated from the heat to concern myself with Malcolm's declaration that he wants to both date me *and* be my friend. That was what girls wished and prayed and hoped for their whole lives. Despite the fact that I had only spent one full day and a train ride with him, this was a very promising step. I didn't even have the energy to text Bethany with this news. I found a cold-air vent in my house and just sat in front of it for a while, periodically shifting angles so the refreshing air could be evenly distributed. After I had thoroughly cooled off, I grabbed my cell phone to see what messages I had waiting for me to answer.

One was from my mother.

MOM: On my way home. What u want 4 dinner?

Grammar in texting wasn't exactly her forte. I was just glad she didn't ask about my response from J.A.M.

Another message was from Bethany.

BETHANY: Hey gurl! Work is boring. Wanna go out this weekend? We could go to bars in Morristown. Oh! Did you hear from my dad's company yet? Have you talked to Malcolm??? Must hear details! Is it hot outside?

It was like she was throwing everything that could possibly be on my mind in my face at the same time. And clearly, she had not been outside yet.

The last text message in my inbox was from Malcolm (excuse my swooning).

> MALCOLM: I'd like to take you on a date. In NYC. Do
> you want to?

Of course, the answer to a question like this coming from Malcolm was always going to be a resounding yes.

I made plans to meet Malcolm for a day-date in New York City for the next weekend. He knew I wasn't so keen on being in the city at night. I was still in suburban mode and not quite ready for urban nightlife yet. While he didn't detail the planned events of our pending city rendezvous, I was sure it would be fantastical. I had no qualms about that.

However, one thing that was worrisome to me at the time was that the end of July was fast approaching and I still had no job prospects or plans to move out of my parents' house, as I had been told were to be my main goals. They didn't want me to rush the process, and yet my parents still wanted me to take on the full adult life experience ASAP. They hadn't given me a set deadline, but I could tell it was soon. With my most recent rejection established and setting in, the idea of continuing a job search for careers in a field I wasn't even slightly qualified for was looking more like a chore than an exciting venture for my future.

I sent Bethany a quick text about my date with Malcolm and received a spirited response that read:

> BETHANY: OOooOOooOO!!!

I declined to reply with more explanation. Instead, I ascended the stairs to my bedroom, opened the door, took a few steps in, and face planted myself into my bed. That led to my curling up into a ball and having a good cry. These were no crocodile tears like I was known for. Rather, they were full on tears of desperation. The pressure that I had been feeling from my parents, and myself for that matter, had been building up since June 27th. No. It had been building up since graduation in May. No. This pressure cooker started in the beginning of senior year when everyone in my class was starting the job hunt or even signing contracts for post-grad jobs or applying to grad school. That would be everyone except for me. I couldn't figure out why I had been so behind schedule on this important stage of my life. I was a smart girl. I studied Philosophy for God sake! I had the smarts of an intellectual and yet I couldn't rationalize finding a career-job for myself. Somehow I had uninvited myself from that party. That was a party of success. The one I relegated myself to was the one of the Peter Pan complexes. I had been told for years that playing on swing sets was for children only – that I was no longer a child, and how I needed to grow up. I was constantly compared to my cousins who had made something of themselves already. Tía Rosa would always brag about her daughter and my cousin Graciela who was in medical school studying to be a surgeon already. She graduated undergrad a year early. She has a great boyfriend and wedding bells seem to be in the future. My family had a way of making me feel like crap. Just because I didn't have ambitions of being a doctor or have some wonderful boyfriend (yet) who wanted to marry me or have such a boring, adult outlook that sucks the fun out of everything, that doesn't make me any less entitled to a life of my own. I needed to remember that. I needed to write that down. But I was still curled up in a ball on my bed with powder blue beaded princess sheets in an almost catatonic state. I wanted this process to be easier. I wanted to get respect from my family. I wanted an adult life as long as I didn't have to compromise my fun side.

Bethany always called me a child under her breath. I would pretend not to hear it, but I would hear it every time. It made me wonder if that was how most people saw me. That was the first time I ever entertained that thought. It certainly didn't feel good to be treated as a child by my peers. I needed to do something about it. Again, I tried to sit up, but I just ended up more attached to the bed. I was still crying and the more I contemplated my state of arrested development, the more tears came out. Crocodile tears didn't work that way. My immediate urge was to go to the swing-set-jungle-gym-apparatus to feel the breeze in my hair and clear my mind. That's when I remembered the oppressive heat. That was also when my parents got home from work. And I was to be the bearer of some news that was sure to be disappointing to the empty-nesters-to-be.

CHAPTER SEVEN

"Do not spoil what you have by desiring what you have not; remember that what you now have was once among the things you only hoped for." – Epicurus

"Requires five years experience," I read under my breath as I scoured the Internet jobs listings. "Nope."

I was on a mission (as per my parents' orders). Unfortunately, my mother and father weren't going to have the house for themselves as soon as they hoped. According to them, since I still lived under their roof, I still had to live by their rules. By that, they meant that I needed to show some more effort in finding a career-job. Quickly. Apparently, going on a job interview and receiving some great, positive feedback wasn't enough to appease these two. So I took to my laptop and the Interwebs to find my dream job that I was actually qualified for and could enjoy. That last part was the clincher.

"Ideal candidate must be both detail oriented and smart. Must be able to keep up with busy boss," I read another description with hope. "Must be located in Stamford, CT." And all hope was gone. There was no way I was moving all the way to Connecticut. New York City was far enough from home for me.

Personally, sitting in my room as a slave to my computer wasn't exactly the way I had envisioned spending the summer before I had to put on my big-girl pants and get a job. Of course, my parents expected me to have been wearing big-girl pants all along. They were disappointed that I wasn't more responsible about securing the next step of my future.

So I continued clicking and searching and typing and reading through job description after job description for about 2 hours. It felt like a wash-rinse-repeat cycle that lasted the whole day. My mind was becoming mush and I needed some sustenance.

My mother was in the kitchen pouring herself a glass of wine.

"How's the search going?" she asked.

"Oh, it's going ... swell."

"You don't need to be sarcastic with me."

I said nothing in response and just rummaged through the fridge looking for something, anything to eat.

"I don't appreciate this silent treatment either," she scolded.

To which I replied (with my face still in the refrigerator), "Do we have any pudding?"

"Josefina," my mother continued. "Just because this is a difficult stage in your life does not give you the liberty to treat everyone around you like they suddenly don't matter. It's all a part of growing up."

I immediately turned to her in reaction to this insult. "Can you answer my question?" I paused. "Please?"

"We don't have any more in the little cups. There's a box of pudding in the pantry. You would have to make it yourself."

"Ugh! Forget it!" I exclaimed and threw up my arms in an over dramatic gesture and began to walk away and up to my room for further online self-torture. It was already 11:30 at night. Another day had come and gone and somehow nothing productive was achieved.

The next morning, I awoke to a text message. My phone buzzed with its super-charged vibration setting that felt like it shook the house. I instantly jolted to sit up in bed though it had a surprising, disorienting effect on me. I sat there with my arms outstretched turning from side to side looking for my phone that was somewhere within the sheets of my bed. After not being able to find it for a minute or so, I started to question my intelligence and then I got out of bed and pulled all the sheets off my bed. It seemed like a good idea at the time. There was a mass of linens on the floor and since the phone had stopped buzzing, all I could do was start searching for a rectangular object within the blue, beaded comforter and various assorted pillows.

"Hallelujah!" I called out rather loudly when I finally found my connection with the world. The buzz was a text from Malcolm.

MALCOLM: What did your parents say?

ME: Better than expected.

I realized I was lucky that my parents didn't ever consider kicking me out to be on my own without an exit plan. At least, I was pretty sure they had never considered that. They wanted me to be at least somewhat prepared for my next steps. I suppose it would be somewhat irresponsible for them to send me out into the world with twenty bucks in my pocket and a kiss goodbye with the optional words of encouragement. If that were the case for me, my father would have said something like, *Buena suerte, Josefina. Good luck out there.* Short and sweet and Spanish.

Still, I wanted to be gainfully employed. I wanted to have a steady job like Bethany and Malcolm. I wanted to live somewhere that would feel like it was mine. I wanted to keep an extra stock of pudding cups for my personal consumption. I wanted a lot of things, but most importantly, I wanted an adult way of life. So naturally, I decided to play on my swing-set-jungle-gym-apparatus.

It was still oppressively hot and humid outside, but the breeze on my face felt so refreshing. As the beads of sweat swept off my face, so did some of the worries I had about this new job search and my future. Honestly, I felt like one of those little kids who gets thrown in the pool and just starts flailing their arms around in order to stay afloat. My lack of a true purpose in life made this process even more difficult. I had no way of narrowing down a location or an occupation. It was as if my parents pushed me into the middle of the ocean and expected me to swim. I was barely treading water. Oh, for the days when water wing floaties were all the rage.

After about a half an hour of swinging and contemplating my life in a mid-air bubble, I returned to my air-conditioned reality. I sat down at my desk, opened up my laptop, leaned on my left arm propped up by my elbow, and started clicking away at the screen. Numerous tabs on my browser linked to job-finding sites at my disposal. I got started plugging away. I applied to 46 jobs in one day. I wasn't even qualified for more than half of them. I knew I needed to start somewhere. However, that somewhere was still undiscovered. My parents wanted me to find a career job and a place to live by summer's end. That was my deadline. I feared that rushing this process was going to leave me alone and unhappy with whatever decision I would be able to make.

I considered biding my time by playing online games while I was supposed to be playing the role of an adult. I didn't feel like an adult though I legally was one for three years already. Growing up never seemed very appealing to me. When I thought of people graduating into adulthood, I imagined holding down a grueling 9 to 5 job in order to support a family with 2.5 kids, lots of bills to pay, and absolutely no fun. Then, if I switched tabs on my browser to any social media site I held an account with, I could see that most of my 452 friends/followers/fans/fiends or whatever you want to freaking call them had careers and lives far more interesting than mine – though at that rate, working at the local diner was looking better than struggling with my lack of focus and drive. At least the diner was a paying establishment. Sitting around playing Tetris in my room was not exactly going to help my bank account. Especially since I've never been any good at Tetris.

After two more days of the incessant torture of writing cover letters and sending out my resume, I got to the point of just sitting and staring at my computer. It was a stare down. I was also starting to wonder if any of these places actually received my e-mails. Then, in the middle of my stare down with my computer, a box popped up on my screen notifying me that I had a new e-mail. Of course I immediately dismissed it as being some spam message from some sketchy site/person/thing trying to sell me some penile-enhancing device/medication/grossness when clearly, I don't have any use for that. Subsequently, after ignoring this message for a few minutes to continue staring down the image of my face that I generated from the internal camera of my laptop, I decided that I lost the glaring game. So I forfeited and hoped that the e-mail waiting for me was filled with news. Good or bad would work. I wasn't being too picky at this point.

Re: Josefina Ruiz Internship Application at Jarvis Advertising & Marketing

Ms. Ruiz,

Although we had previously informed you that all of the spots in the internship program at Jarvis Advertising & Marketing were occupied, recently, there has been an opening. We would like to invite you to join our team in a paid internship this fall.

Your standout interview and academic strong suits proved to be very impressive to our judging committee. Our internship program in New York City will offer you a world of unmatched experience in the field of advertising and marketing. If you are still interested in this position, please contact me at your earliest convenience.

I look forward to hearing from you.

Best,
Donna Majesco
Public Relations Director
Jarvis Advertising & Marketing

The fact that this message came at the point where I was on the verge of going crazy was a godsend. I needed something to lift my spirits and get me out of the unemployment funk I was in. This was it. I had a great opportunity and I was going to take it. But first, to celebrate!

Of course, text messages went out to Bethany and Malcolm. My parents were at work so I figured I would let the news simmer until they arrived at home. So I did a little happy dance. Well, I did a lot of happy dancing, which consisted of me playing Britney Spears off my computer and jumping around like a fool.

I then responded to Donna Majesco's e-mail:

> Hello Ms. Majesco,
> I would be thrilled to accept the internship position at Jarvis Advertising & Marketing. When would I start? I currently live in Bellcastle, New Jersey so I'll need to make arrangements to live in closer proximity to the office. Also, if you could disclose the pay wage/monthly income I can expect, that would be very helpful. If there are any other details to the internship that you can share with me, I would really appreciate it. This is very exciting and I cannot wait to be a part of the team!
>
> Thank you,
> Josefina Ruiz

About an hour later, Donna Majesco wrote back to me and attached a 32-page document that included any and all possible details about the internship program that I would potentially have any questions about. Page 7 addressed the money part of the internship. According to the document, I would not be receiving an hourly wage, but rather a weekly stipend for my work. That stipend was $257 leaving me with $1,028 monthly. I wasn't sure why they didn't round it off to $250, but I wasn't going to swindle myself out of seven extra dollars a month. I honestly wasn't even sure if that monthly income was a lot or a little. In order to earn that income, I was required to work in the office five days a week from 9 a.m. to 5 p.m. I was also expected to attend after hours office events. This booklet also contained several pages on how to be a model intern. While I had never been an intern before in my life, I decided to skip over those eight pages. They were very clear that all housing arrangements had to be made independently by the intern. Crap. My first day for the program would be in about a month on August 26. I needed to get working on finding a place to live. *Rapidamente.*

Somehow my excitement over now having a paid internship within my grasp was quickly overshadowed by the fact that I had nowhere to live. I conducted a general search for apartments in New York City. What came up astounded me. A 350 square-foot studio apartment on East 82nd Street would cost $1,600 a month! I didn't know exactly where East 82nd Street was in Manhattan, but I knew that $1,600 was way out of my budget. Clearly I was going to need roommates. However, I had never lived with a roommate before. Living in the same house with my parents for 21 years didn't really count. This was going to be an unforeseen challenge that I was not exactly looking forward to. Some people would call this a new stage in life. I called it the wake-up-and-grow-up stage. I had a feeling Peter Pan never encountered this kind of problem.

My Princeton research skills turned out to be very handy. First, I started looking into the different neighborhoods in Manhattan. I decided that I was already afraid of that borough; I wasn't about to venture into Brooklyn or Queens or any of the other boroughs I knew absolutely nothing about. My ignorance would be my folly.

Seeing that I was completely hopeless at looking for a New York City apartment on my own, I decided to enlist the assistance of Malcolm, who I knew lived in a two-bedroom apartment in Manhattan with two other guys. Apparently, both bedrooms were occupied and the living room was partitioned off as an extra bedroom for the third guy. He said it wasn't so ideal for the living room dude, but they let him pay less in monthly rent as a tradeoff. I called Malcolm to see if he had any advice on how to find a decent priced apartment and a roommate who wouldn't be a total pain to live with.

"Well first, you have to figure out what areas of the city you would be willing to live in," Malcolm advised.

I had already come to the conclusion that since I didn't know the city, my lack of familiarity left me with the Museum of Modern Art, Madison Square Park, and Penn Station. Clearly, those were not viable residential options. After explaining this predicament to him, he suggested that we substitute our upcoming weekend date as a day date to show me around the city.

"It will be great," he said enthusiastically. "I can show you some of the different neighborhoods. It will help you get a better idea of where you might want to live."

"I guess," I said with a tone of fear and anxiety in my voice.

"Think of it this way: we'll get to see each other and you can explore the city with someone you actually like. It's not as scary as it seems."

So we made plans for me to come to the city via train that Saturday morning in order to have a full day of exploration through the various corners of New York City. Malcolm assured me this would also be an amazing day date that I would not forget.

CHAPTER EIGHT

"Love is a serious mental disease." – Plato

I never actually had a realistic crush. Sure, I obsessed over a lot of movie stars and famous musicians. And of course I thought there were some hot guys on the Princeton water polo and soccer teams. My infatuation with Chris Brady in junior year Political Philosophy Seminar lasted far beyond one semester, but he was dead set on becoming a State Senator or Congressman or something political and official. He had a five-year plan. And I had less than a plan. So that was not a realistic crush either. Malcolm, on the other hand, was a realistic crush. First of all, it was evident that he actually liked me as more than a friend. That was a big step. He was eager for me to move to New York City so I could be closer to him and so we wouldn't have to rely solely on text messages and online chatting to stay in touch. Seeing the other person face to face was preferable. Maybe he would want to be my boyfriend. That would be something. Look out world! Josefina is going to have a boyfriend for the first time in her life and he doesn't only live in a poster on her wall. He is real. And his name is Malcolm.

I entertained this thought the whole train ride to New York. I kept thinking about how I would act when I met Malcolm at Penn Station. I considered different options. What if when I saw him, I ran up to him and wrapped my arms around him and kicked my leg up like they always do in the movies? I thought that was a good first step, however,

I forgot to take into account all of the droves of people roaming the halls of Penn Station, desensitized and full of purpose. In the little time I had spent in New York City, one thing I noticed was that New Yorkers can really book it. I felt like a snail trailing the crowd that raced by. I had a feeling that these people with walking gusto were likely going to get in the way of master plan *numero uno*.

Another option was one that was a little risky. My second thought was to bob and weave through the mass of commuters and when standing directly in front of Malcolm, give him a little kiss on the cheek. I thought it would be sweet. I texted Bethany about this idea seeking helpful guidance of any kind. I had never kissed a guy on the lips. I was a late bloomer in that department – so sue me. Bethany thought the classic cheek kiss would be sweet. She said it would show I was interested in him in a romantic way, rather than leave him in the dark thinking he was in the "Friend Zone." Nobody looking to connect wants to be in the "Friend Zone." However, I was fairly sure that Malcolm had at least an inkling that I liked him as more than a friend, so kissing him on the cheek as a "Hello" would only solidify that fact in the event there was any question about it. Then, Bethany did say that if I did in fact really like Malcolm and wanted to continue seeing him and possibly have the seeing turn into a relationship, I would have to "seal the deal," as she said. By that, she meant that I would have to bite the bullet, leave my fears behind, and dive right in. Translation: kiss him at the end of the date.

BETHANY: Leave him wanting more. ;)

That was easier said than done.

BETHANY: Practice your kissy face :*

I was on a train. Although nobody was sitting next to me on this trip to the city, I felt rather uncomfortable practicing my kissy face with conductors walking past and checking on passengers. While mostly everyone was completely enticed and occupied by their phones and other forms of addictive technology, I decided to turn and face the window next to me so I could begin my kissy face session in whatever reflection I could get from the scratched and sun drenched view. To say it was a successful session would be a huge overstatement. I spent most of my intimate moment with a window reflection with one eye on the aisle, checking if I was in the clear. I hoped nobody noticed my attempts to essentially make out with myself. On a train. I was not exactly proud of it.

When I got off the train, I took a deep breath and attempted to find the street exit that led to 32nd Street and Seventh Avenue. Clearly, I was not familiar with the halls of Penn Station and I was already destined to get pushed around and be lost. That is exactly what happened. Somehow, I ended up in the Long Island Railroad wing although I arrived via New Jersey Transit. All I wanted was to find a sign labeled with the streets I needed to find so I could meet up with Malcolm. After wandering through various bustling corridors that all looked eerily similar, I eventually found a sign that directed me to a street. I was pretty sure it wasn't the intersection I was supposed to be at, but at least I would be on the street and beyond the underground hustle and bustle. Oh, how wrong I was. I made my way up the steep steps and walked into the sun at 33rd Street and Eighth Avenue. People rushed by me as soon as I made the first step onto the hot pavement. There were so many pedestrians walking in different directions and populating the sidewalk; all I could do was attach myself to a wall. I took out my phone and called Malcolm so he could come and find me. He asked what streets I was near and to wait there for him. I felt bad that I always seemed to get lost when I had plans to meet with him. I also wondered if I could still manage to make my original greeting – upon seeing Malcolm – a reality. Anxiety began to set in.

I looked around frantically for a few minutes that felt like an hour hoping to spot Malcolm in the crowd. Eventually, he showed up beside me as I was nervously looking in the other direction. He poked me on the shoulder and I screamed as I turned around to face him.

"Oh my God!" I shrieked and almost smacked him in the face.

To be fair, Malcolm was apologetic and did give me a big hug to try and calm me down. I was sure he could feel my heart beating loud and fast over that terrifying welcome.

"You got here on your own!" he said.

"I did, didn't I?" I said proudly.

Then, he asked if I was hungry, which I was. He surprisingly took my hand and led me to a hot dog stand on the corner.

"What is this?" I asked skeptically.

"This is food. It's cheap food, but it's the fuel of New York," he responded confidently. "You do like hot dogs, right?"

I stood there looking at him dumbfounded. I had eaten from hot dog stands at the Jersey Shore, but somehow I trusted those hot dogs over these in the city. I actually worried about how sanitary policies applied to these food stands that were situated on street corners.

"What do you want on your hot dog?" Malcolm asked.

As a girl with a discerning taste palate, I just said, "just ketchup and mustard, please." I didn't need sauerkraut or any other relish, especially since I wasn't exactly sure if I would even enjoy a New York City hot dog.

"Here," Malcolm handed me a hot dog with ketchup and mustard.

I inspected it for a minute until he asked, "Are you going to look at it? Or are you going to eat it?"

I shot him a smile and took a bite out of my first city street hot dog. It was actually pretty good. I started to wonder if New York had some more pleasant surprises for me.

Malcolm motioned for me to follow him.

"Don't get lost!" he called out to me.

That's kind of an opposite day statement to make to me. If you advise me not to get lost, I will probably get lost anyway.

He was walking so fast. And I was so nervous about the possibility of getting lost somewhere in this city. I didn't know where to look. There were billboards, signs that told you when to walk or not to walk, cars, people, and stores with extravagant window displays surrounding us. Of course, it was overwhelming. I started noticing the numbers on the street signs going up.

"Where are we going, Malcolm?" I asked.

"You'll see. It's not too much farther."

I was still confused and my head was spinning. Soon enough, I started to notice even more droves of people filling the streets in the direction we were approaching. The space between each person on the street got tighter as we walked. My arms were bumped into so many times that I felt bruised. The noise level rose with each step and that's saying a lot since we were in the middle of New York City, where it's always noisy. Or so I'm told. I still had no idea where we were going. We reached West 40th Street. I wasn't paying much attention to the avenue sign. Soon enough, the crowd grew to a monstrous size and the pace increased to a walking sprint. I knew immediately that I was not wearing the right shoes for this type of occasion.

Malcolm stopped at a corner. "Here we are!"

"Where are we?" I asked hesitantly, looking around like a lost little girl.

"We're in Times Square!" he said with as much enthusiasm as a radio announcer on a caffeine high.

"Okay," I said as I looked around. "Why is it so crowded? It didn't feel this crowded five blocks ago."

"That's because it's all over-commercialized and every tourist in New York comes here. Millions of people everyday. But it's fun! There's a lot to do and see here."

It was sweet how he was trying to convince me that this was a good place for me to jump into on my first real excursion into the city. So we continued on. But first, he took hold of my hand so I wouldn't get lost in the mass of people. *Slick move,* I thought. He was like a hand holding ninja.

He led me through the crowd as we bobbed and weaved past some guys dressed up as Cookie Monster and Elmo, tourists in safari gear decked out with super-zoom lens cameras, and a bunch of lost people who just needed to get out of the way. Malcolm pointed out some landmarks to me like some Broadway theaters, the Bubba Gump restaurant, and the MTV studio building. But what really interested me was the colossal Toys "R" Us located smack dab in the middle of all the action. I was getting a little overwhelmed with the traffic, people constantly asking, "Hey! Wanna see a comedy show?" and the video billboards calling out for my attention. When I found a sort of clearing in the sea of tourists, I grabbed Malcolm and made a run for it. He was surprised by my sudden burst of energy after having most of it drained by the incessant stop and go on the sidewalks. I pulled him past a group of almost 20 tourists from somewhere who all simultaneously stopped to take a picture of a street sign. We inched our way through the crowd attempting to fit in the revolving door and finally, we had arrived. There was a life size Barbie house and a Lego section, but what was most impressive to me was the giant Ferris Wheel in the middle of the store. So of course, I grabbed for Malcolm's hand again – only this time it was his arm – and we were off to the line for the Ferris Wheel. Then, we were told we needed tickets to actually ride it. Malcolm was sweet enough to buy tickets for us, which was good because my bank account was looking pretty low. So we waited in line as these two 10 year-old girls in front of us played the "I'm not touching you" game. They ended up getting on the Ferris Wheel still playing that game.

Eventually, it was our turn. The Ferris Wheel operator welcomed us in a very droll voice.

"Welcome to Toys 'R' Us where toy dreams come true," he said with an unaffected tone.

We had the privilege of riding in the Mr. and Mrs. Potato Head cab. I was about to jump out of my skin from excitement.

"You seem really happy right now," Malcolm observed matter of factly.

"I love Ferris Wheels!" I suddenly knew how Bethany felt back when she had all those Red Bull and vodkas. I actually felt like dancing like a gummy bear. And all I ate was a hot dog!

I tried playing down my excitement, but I was on a Ferris Wheel in the middle of a Toys 'R' Us store located in the heart of New York City. The child in me was having a field day. One thing that also occurred to me was that although the store was ridiculously loud and crowded with tourists looking for an authentic New York experience, sitting at the top of that Ferris Wheel with Malcolm felt like quietest place in the whole city. We were alone in this Mr. Potato Head cab soaking up the love that Mr. and Mrs. Potato Head have for each other. By osmosis, we were destined to fall in love. I started hearing the frogs from *The Little Mermaid* singing "Kiss The Girl" in my head. I was fully aware that this was not actually happening in real life, but it was a fantasy that didn't seem so far-fetched – except for the singing frogs part.

Malcolm told me about his school experience at Montclair State University while studying environmental sciences. He talked about his parents and his siblings – one brother and one sister. He was in the middle. We had discussed some basic parts of our life on that first train ride together, but the Ferris Wheel brought about an even more intimate environmental science for Malcolm to study.

After sitting at the top of the wheel for a few minutes, we descended back to the beginning. I was worried that our ride was over already after spending 14 dollars on each ticket. So I made a motion to the hipster dude who was operating the ride to let us go for another round. If we stayed, he would hate his life and if we got off the ride, he would probably still hate his life. I would hate having to let these bratty kids on a ride and never have the opportunity to ride it myself, too. So I had some sympathy for this guy.

Malcolm and I continued our conversation about life and where we wanted to be in five years. He said he wanted to be a park manager at Central Park in five years. That was his plan.

"I love working at Madison Square Park. It's really picturesque and there are a lot of great events to help manage, but Central Park has it all. It's the big leagues. That's where I want to be."

I was glad to hear he had goals and knew what he wanted to do with his life. He wanted to make a difference with the Central Park Conservancy making sure the land remained a beautiful landmark for the city. I respected him for that. Malcolm had goals. I, on the other hand, was completely lost. Although I had a paid internship waiting for me at the end of August, I wasn't even sure if advertising and marketing was the career for me. Before I honestly considered that line of work, I had applied to just about every company that was hiring, with all deliberate speed, I was also missing a very important detail of the plan: a place to live on a rather small budget.

"You're going to need roommates," Malcolm said.

I knew he was right, but it was a fact that I dreaded. Having never lived in close quarters with anyone except for my mother and father, this roommate thing was going to be a challenge. Aside from not knowing my way around the city at all, I was bound to get lost, swindled, and stuck with some psycho who doesn't know what good hygiene is. Smelliness would not be acceptable.

After the third go-around on the Ferris Wheel (I think the hipster guy thought I was cute or something), Malcolm and I decided to explore the gigantic store. Of course, our first stop was the life-size dollhouse dedicated to all things Barbie. On the "front lawn walk" to the house, we were pushed and almost thrown off balance a few times by some eager kids, but I paid no attention to that when there were all sorts of variations of Barbie dolls surrounding me. I felt like a kid in a wondrous play land and it turned out that that was exactly what I was in that moment.

"I had no idea you liked toy stores so much," Malcolm mentioned to me as we made the excursion into the three-story dollhouse filled with even more goodies for me to get distracted by. Clearly, there was so much more he needed to learn about me.

Malcolm was always good at observing things about me. He observed me like I was a fascinating science experiment that he couldn't let out of his sight. This would be a red flag to any other girl, considering I had not even been on a real date before. Therefore, I never took much notice to his observations. They flew right over my head – kind of like a lot of Bethany's jokes.

We reached the top level of the house, and I wanted to reach out and say something declarative like, "I'm the Barbie queen of the world!" but I knew that would embarrass Malcolm so I decided against that.

Eventually, we made our way out of the super toy store. Malcolm made the decision that it was far too hot outside to walk everywhere. We would take the subway. I knew he wanted to show me the city, but this seemed like a good idea. I certainly didn't want my body to melt and my feet to hurt and my hair to become a frizzy mess. So we braved our way through the throngs of people and headed to the Times Square subway station. He helped me purchase my first MetroCard. I almost felt like a New Yorker just from holding one of those pieces of plastic that united the city. Trying to get my rhythm swiping that card for entry into the subway system was embarrassing though. I must have spent a whole five minutes that felt like a lifetime trying to swipe that card. I was either too slow, too fast, or didn't realize the machine was beeping at me to mean "GO!" rather than "YOU SUCK!" Malcolm even tried swiping the card for me. That didn't work either. I did it by myself after holding up the line and annoying every person behind me.

When I got to the other side, an older man leaned toward me and said, "You don't come here very often, do you?" which really creeped me out since Bethany said the exact same thing to me just a few weeks before. Bizarre.

We descended steep steps to the boiling underground world of the subway system. I think I sweat more in the tunnels than I was sweating up at street level. Malcolm said we had to take the downtown N train. Immediately after we found the right platform, the N train arrived and we got on the extremely packed train car. It wasn't bad enough that it was a hot summer day so everyone was sweaty; a malodorous smell was reeking from the people packed in like sardines.

"Malcolm," I asked. "Which stop are we getting off at?"

I was starting to be bothered by the lack of personal space on the train. It wasn't like walking through a crowd in Times Square; this was like those games they played in the 1960s trying to fit as many people as possible in a Volkswagen Beetle. Although there was air conditioning, it did not even begin to quell the pungent air.

"We're going to Union Square," Malcolm responded. "It's four stops from here. We're on a local train."

The subway train doors opened at 34th Street (I knew this because a nice, automated man's voice told me so) and hot air emanated from the station into the air-conditioned car. People hurried into the train car, pushing to get a spot in the remains of the available personal space. Then came the strollers, which took up the space of three people. I was backed into a corner holding onto Malcolm as the nice, automated man's voice said "Stand clear of the closing doors." As the doors closed, I felt trapped and a woman who looked like she hadn't showered in days kept bumping into me as the train rocked back and forth.

"The woman next to me keeps touching my arm," I told Malcolm as discretely as possible.

"It's a crowded train. We're all squished next to each other. As long as she doesn't steal anything from your bag, you'll be okay," he said rationally.

Of course, as the one with a degree in philosophy, I had to be the completely irrational one.

"I don't like being touched, though," I whispered to him. Apparently, I was not stealth enough with that whisper. I was loud enough to be heard by Malcolm, but apparently sound travels on these trains and two women near me had this urge to comment on what I had just whispered for Malcolm's ears only.

> WOMAN 1: How you gonna say you don't like being touched? You're on the subway! You're gonna get touched!

> WOMAN 2: True that.

Then they laughed. I wanted to get off the train and hide away somewhere. To me, it felt like that day in second grade when I made a really loud and stinky fart during the middle of my presentation on my beautiful paint creation from art class. It went like this: "And so the rainbow has lots of colors. They all mean something different. Red is my favorite. It's my favorite color. My lunchbox is red and my socks are red and–" FART! My face turned a bright shade of my favorite color and from that day on, just about every time someone let one loose, it was blamed on me. They called me Farty Josie until the end of fourth grade.

The moral of the lesson with the two ladies on the subway was that if I was going to move to New York, I was going to need learn how to keep some comments to myself. The lesson for my second grade embarrassment was to hold it in until you can go to the bathroom.

We arrived at the Union Square subway stop. Malcolm held my hand so I wouldn't get lost trying to find the exit. I felt like I was more of a liability than a date. I didn't know how to act with him. He kept trying to protect me so I could see what the city had to offer me rather than let it scare me. The heat downstairs in the station was almost unbearable, but walking up to the surface was insufferable. The sun was oppressive and it felt like the temperature had risen, like, 10 degrees. It was one of those deceiving days where the weather forecaster would say, "Today will be a scorcher! Actual temperature is 80, but feels like 102 degrees. Enjoy the beautiful day!" I always hated when they reported nonsense like that. Sure, I will enjoy this beautiful day – indoors, with the air conditioning pumped way up. I'm Puerto Rican, so the heat doesn't necessarily bother me like it would other people, but when it's too hot, it is just too hot.

The first thing Malcolm showed me in Union Square was the park. We took a little walk through under the refreshing shade of the trees with overhanging branches along the main walkway. It was a cute park, but without a playground and a swing set, it didn't quite meet my biased park ranking system.

"How far is Madison Square Park from here?" I asked Malcolm during our stroll.

"It's only a few blocks from here," he answered.

"Okay," I said defeated.

Union Square Park was starting to look pretty boring to me.

"Now the next place we're going is not a square," Malcolm hinted to me.

I was thrilled. "I was starting to wonder if whoever planned out Manhattan was all about squares. I mean, so far I've been to Times *Square*, Union *Square*, and Madison *Square* Park."

"There's also Washington Square Park, Tompkins Square Park. And don't forget Madison Square Garden, which is not a park at all and has no gardens as far as I know," Malcolm cleverly quipped.

"So where is this *circle* place?" I asked.

"It's actually quite a few blocks from here, but it seems to be cooling off a little so maybe we can walk up there so you can see the city."

I stopped walking and looked at him quizzically.

"We can stop and take breaks in air conditioned places along the way," Malcolm responded.

"How many blocks are we talking here?"

"It's on 59th Street and Columbus Avenue. It's on the west side. It will be worth it. I promise."

"We'll take breaks?" I asked him as a test. I was going to walk with him regardless. Honestly, at that point, I would walk, run, jump, and skip across the earth with Malcolm. He was the sweetest guy and although he didn't know me very well at that point, he wasn't completely turned off by my Peter Pan syndrome. I really wanted to kiss him and I hoped my kissy face practice session would help. I actually started sweating from places on my body that I didn't even know existed – not only because of the heat – but because I was so nervous I would say something awkward. Is that what love feels like? I had never felt anything like that before.

After a few blocks, I could feel that single drop of sweat travel down my spine. My armpits were sticking to the straps of the canvas bag I had securely on my shoulder. It was a very disconcerting sensation to feel like I was melting from the inside out. My hair stuck to my forehead in an extremely unattractive way. I kept using my arm to keep the damp strands from falling in my eyes. I was quite unsuccessful. The long, black strands clumped together whenever a refreshing breeze blew in, which only made them land strangely on my face. I was not exactly the vision of perfection I hoped to be. Epic fail.

Malcolm struck up conversation to make the walk go past quicker. He asked me about my parents, which I was not exactly eager to discuss, but regardless I shared their story. I wasn't enthusiastic talking about their tactics for getting me to move out just so they could be empty nesters. Surprisingly, Malcolm wasn't as disappointed in them as I was.

"I'm sure they had the best intentions for doing that," he explained. "I mean, your parents gave you that initiative to get yourself together and live an adult life. What would you be doing if they hadn't done that?"

His analysis of my parents' master plan made sense. If they hadn't surprised me with that bomb of a birthday present, I would probably be sitting on my swing-set-jungle-gym-apparatus that I had been playing on since I was a kid. Not that there's anything wrong with that. Or I would be sitting inside with air conditioning clicking through social media accounts, watching some romantic comedy movies, or frankly, just being bored. It's just unlikely that I would be doing anything particularly productive for my life. So in that light, Malcolm was actually right. Regardless of who was right, I still resented how my parents handled that situation.

Since Malcolm asked first, it was my turn to ask him a question. My first instinct was to ask if he had a girlfriend, but I quickly decided against that since clearly, if he had a girlfriend, he probably would have mentioned her by now and wouldn't be on a day date with me at the moment. I wasn't experienced with the whole "dating" thing, but I knew asking a dumb question like that would have been really weird. I was the queen of being awkward, but I didn't necessarily want to throw that card out there at that point. After wracking my brain for almost two blocks, I thought of something.

"Ooh! Ooh! Okay. I have one," I said emphatically. "You live in the city, right? So when we met that day on the train and I was going to my interview, why were you even on the train in Jersey?"

He paused for a moment. "The truth?"

"Yeah. I don't want to hear any stories about how you saved some guy from a fire and how your town gave you the key to the city and so you had to go home for the ceremony."

"Wow. That would have been a good story to tell. Mine isn't nearly that interesting."

"Oh?"

"Yeah. See, my mom's a little bit overwhelming to deal with. She's really sweet and cares far too much about her kids, but, well, my parents have been divorced for five years now and she likes to go out on dates a lot. I don't think she's ever really gotten over my dad though. It was really tough for her. The divorce. Actually, whenever I'm home, she always comments to me about how I should never be like my father. Anyway, my mom was going on a date that night with some guy she met online. This was the second date so she was really excited about it. My little sister, Keri, is ten years old and she was going to have some friends over for a sleepover. My mom needed me to supervise while she was out for the night."

"Okay. So we both have weird relationships with our parents then."

"Yeah. I guess so," Malcolm said in a deflated tone.

There was a silence for a moment or two. It wasn't good silence. It was awkward silence. *No me gusta silencio.*

"It looks like there's a coffee shop across the street," I chimed in to break the silence. "I think it's time for one of those breaks."

"Good suggestion. I could really go for some ice cold water right about now," Malcolm got on the bandwagon.

I figured the cool air of the indoors would cool Malcolm's heels. Obviously, it was beyond sweltering, but being Puerto Rican, I could take a little heat.

We cooled off and headed back on the trail towards this Columbus Circle place Malcolm kept gabbing on about. Since we started our journey on the East side of town, we had to make our way to the West side of Manhattan. Malcolm suggested we take the route along Broadway. I didn't know the difference between taking Broadway or taking the West Side Highway so I followed him blindly. We crossed through Herald Square, which was a claustrophobic mess, and Times Square again, which was an even more claustrophobic mess. I was hyper aware of my surroundings. Part of me was worried someone was going to steal my green canvas bag that was resting comfortably on my shoulder. I didn't have anything particularly valuable in it, but I was conscious that some dumb thief could try and grab it. They would be quite disappointed in their acquisition and it would completely ruin my day. I had a map of New York City, my phone that was worth peanuts, my wallet containing only 20 dollars, a train ticket back to Jersey, car keys for my ancient car, and a MetroCard loaded with 10 dollars. This would be the ultimate womp womp heist. I hoped no stupid and desperate New Yorkers would take that chance with me. My date with Malcolm was going so well. I didn't want any womp womp moments.

I took in the world around me. I knew I should have been more intrigued by the fashionable shops that lined Broadway as we headed uptown, but somehow I wasn't. I wasn't exactly the most fashionable person. Honestly, a tank top, shorts, and sandals were my go-to summer ensemble. I didn't try so hard to impress people with my clothes. I tried to use my brain powers to make an impression. My dad always said I was a smart cookie. Since when did cookies need to be fashionable? I hoped that New York would accept my style or lack thereof, but I had a feeling that would have to change too.

There was a couple walking in front of us as we made it to 50th Street. They seemed so in love. With them as a model, whenever the girl glanced over at her boyfriend, I would glance over at Malcolm. I noticed Malcolm glance back at me. One thing the couple was doing that we were not was holding hands. I dreaded this moment. It was about time for the hand holding to begin. Malcolm and I were getting along famously and we walked in stride telling stories and laughing. We barely even noticed how hot it was outside. I kept looking down at my left hand and Malcolm's right hand. We had been walking side by side for more than a mile and a half. Maybe he was just shy. Maybe he didn't want to make a hasty move. Maybe he wasn't really that into me. I rationalized the hell out of the situation and it didn't do any good. Blast my degree in philosophy! When was that degree ever going to actually help me? It didn't occur to me that I could make the first move and grab his hand as we were walking. He beat me to the punch. Just as I turned away to look at a tea shop on the corner of Broadway and West 58th Street, Malcolm held my hand in a romantic way for the first time. A total sneak attack. I looked down at our entwined hands to make sure this was really happening. If I could have pinched myself without looking like a complete weirdo, I would have. Instead, I had to rely on my senses to prove the reality of the gesture. Then, I looked up at Malcolm to see his reaction. He had the biggest smile on his face. He knew he just pulled off a ninja move and he was damn proud of it. I had to give him credit for that; I certainly wasn't brave enough to reach for his hand first. This whole situation had me writing text messages to Bethany rapid fire in my mind. I couldn't figure out if she would laugh or continually say, "aw." Either way, I'm sure she had never experienced such a sweet, romantic gesture as that in all her years of dating. This was a Nicholas Sparks book territory moment and it was happening in real life! I still had to keep my focus sharp, though. Bethany did say that if I really do like him, I would have to seal the night with a kiss. Eye on the prize. However, I was sure I would need to be the first to make that move and that was absolutely terrifying.

"Here we are!" Malcolm said emphatically for the second time in an almost four hour time frame.

I looked around for a moment as we arrived at wherever we were.

"We're at Columbus Circle!" he answered the question I didn't have to actually ask.

Just as promised, Columbus Circle was in fact a circle with a towering statue of Christopher Columbus as the centerpiece.

"Oh. I see! The place you said wasn't a square! Got it," I assured him I was on the same page. "It's very pretty. I like the statue."

"It's a really great place. The best part is that the park is right here."

"Central Park?" I took an educated guess based on the street sign I saw a block before that read "Central Park West."

"Yep!"

We ventured into Central Park with interlocked fingers. I almost got run over by a bike rider in my attempt to cross over to the pedestrian walkway. A part of me really wanted to say, "Hey! I'm walking here!" like they say in the movies, but I was too afraid some angry New Yorker would actually run me over with a bike if I did that. So I kept my mouth shut. Malcolm and I started strolling on the tree-lined walkway. I was in wonderment with the grandeur of the park.

"How big is Central Park, Malcolm?"

"I'm pretty sure it's over 700 acres. It's huge. There's so much to see and do here. It's actually really exhausting to walk even most of the park in one day. So we can't see everything today. I just wanted you to experience a little bit to start."

"What's your favorite part of the park?" I asked.

"Hmm," Malcolm considered my question for a few moments. "I don't know that I can really answer that. My favorite? Right now, I'm probably gonna say Bethesda Fountain. It's featured in probably, like, every New York movie, but that never diminishes its beauty."

"Where is it in the park?"

"It's right in the middle of the park. Smack dab in the middle."

"Is that far from where we are right now? I'd like to see it. You can tell me about it as much as you want, but I'd like to see why it's your favorite for myself," I said sincerely. "And then I'll decide if it's worth being a favorite," I joked.

"Oh, it's worth it," he chuckled. "It's a walk, though."

"Well lucky for us, I came prepared wearing walking shoes," I said as I looked down at my sandals.

I didn't really want to walk an even longer distance, but like Malcolm, I loved parks. I always felt at home in parks – swing sets or no swing sets. Actually, Malcolm informed me that it's generally against policy to play on swing sets in New York City parks as an adult. Sometimes I could forget that I was an adult. I celebrated my 18th birthday over dinner at my favorite restaurant in Bellcastle with Bethany and my parents. My 21st birthday was kind of a bust. I didn't even have cake! What kind of a birthday doesn't have cake? It doesn't matter how old you are – a birthday without cake to celebrate with isn't a true birthday. Perhaps that was why I was having such trouble coming to terms with adulthood. Then again, maybe it was that my parents babied me my whole life. That could explain a lot. Regardless of my questionable status in adulthood, I was convinced that the first step of growing up was to admit the problem to myself. I had already done that, so I was waiting for the second step of growing up to come to me as a sign. That was going to be harder to find than I thought.

Malcolm and I started walking in the direction of mid-park. Surprisingly, I felt energized by the trek, but Malcolm was running out of steam. I could see him perspiring heavily to the point that the hair on his head was drenched and he was having trouble keeping the sweat out of his eyes. I spotted an empty bench in a tree-shaded section of the walkway for us to take a breather.

"We don't have to go all the way to Bethesda Fountain if it's too much. Is it that far from here?" I inquired.

Malcolm wiped his forehead with his arm and like a man, said, "Nah. It's okay. It's near 72nd Street. We're at, like, 63rd Street. I think. But I'm okay. I'm good. Let's keep going."

He was clearly not in his best form. I suggested visiting another favorite of his that was perhaps closer to our current location.

"Hmm... Actually," he considered. "You know what's close to here?"

"No. I don't know."

"There's a carousel in the park," Malcolm said.

Now he was speaking my language.

"And adults can go on it. You have to pay a few bucks to ride it, but we can ride it."

"Is it far from here?"

"It's actually in the same direction we've been heading in – just not as far uptown. It's very do-able."

"Carousel sounds awesome! Let's go!" I jumped up from the bench with as much excitement as I had when I got my acceptance letter from Princeton.

After giving Malcolm a few moments to cool off and rest up, we walked on toward this amazing carousel he spoke of. I hoped he wasn't just pulling my chain, telling me about this fantastical carousel in the middle of Central Park to leave me disappointed about it. That would be a recipe for a super sad face from Josefina. Eventually, we made it to the pavilion the carousel was housed in. It was just as majestic as I hoped it would be. It looked like one of the carousels they have at boardwalk amusement parks down at the Jersey Shore, only this one was a million times prettier. The painted horses went around and around, making me smile from ear to ear. In my mind, I was instantly transformed into a five year-old. All I wanted to do was ride one of the pretty painted horses. Malcolm wasn't quite as overwhelmed with joy as I was, but he was enthralled nonetheless.

As we made it to the front of the line, we paid our fare to ride the carousel, and chose two horses situated beside each other. I held onto the pole attached to the rainbow color painted pony and looked over at Malcolm on his white horse with a blue and green mane and tail. Such a boy color choice. I was as wide-eyed as when we were in the Toys 'R' Us just a few hours earlier. I could barely contain my excitement about the three minute long carousel ride I was about to experience.

"Oh my God! I'm so glad we did this, Malcolm!" I called to him over the loud carnival music that played as we started the ride.

"I'm glad you're having a good time, Josefina."

"Are you kidding? This is the best date ever!" I said, completely forgetting that this happened to be my *first* date ever. Regardless, Malcolm didn't know that and so he smiled bigger than when he held my hand.

After our excursion in Central Park, it was time for me to get back on a train to Bellcastle. Wisely, we took the subway from Columbus Circle down to Penn Station. Malcolm held my hand the whole subway train ride. It wasn't a particularly long ride downtown, but I figured his holding my hand was a territorial thing – kind of like how dogs pee on everything. He was marking what was his and I was perfectly fine with that – so long as he didn't pee on me. That would be really excessive. It was getting dark outside and by the time I arrived at the train station, the sky was in twilight mode. You couldn't see the stars (it was New York City), but you could definitely see the moon in the dusk.

"Well," I started to say goodbye to a wonderful guy on a wonderful evening. "Malcolm," I spoke in one-word spurts out of nervousness. "This." Pause. "Has been." Pause. "Really." Pause. "Amazing." I let out all the air I had trapped inside my lungs.

"I had a really good time, too," Malcolm said in a full sentence. "We should do this again."

"I'd really love that," I managed to push my fear down.

Then, Malcolm took a step closer. And so I took a step closer. He shuffled his feet even closer. And so I did, too. I knew this was it. I had seen it in movies. It was going to happen. It was inevitable at this point. We locked eyes. This was it. I took the plunge into the kiss. I thought of my kissy face practice and remembered to pucker up hoping I could aim my lips with my eyes closed. And she shoots – and she misses! My lips sort of collided with his nose. That would be a foul in basketball. Malcolm didn't call it as a penalty, though.

"Let's try that again," he said with a keen smile.

So we did. And I scored! Two points for me! No, that was definitely a three pointer. Watching all those romantic comedies during the day while my parents were at work definitely paid off in the end. Who could say I wasn't on task? I was researching important data to prepare for my future as an adult. That's exactly what I started feeling like: an adult. That had to have been step two in the growing up process. The sign came to me and I followed through with a kiss.

I had to catch my train back home. So I practiced with one more goodbye kiss to Malcolm. That one swished. I felt like I was floating as I found a seat on the New Jersey-bound train. As any girl would do after a first date, I texted my best friend, Bethany, with a play by play of the entire day. I was so happy, it didn't even occur to me that the date turned out to be all about New York City parks and that I barely saw any of the neighborhoods I would be potentially looking to live in. Somehow that just ended up as a minor detail as I relaxed on cloud nine all the way back home.

CHAPTER NINE

"Change in all things is sweet." – Aristotle

I spent the next week furiously looking for apartments and looking for roommates on the Internet. If I wasn't doing either of those things, I was either texting, calling, or online chatting with Malcolm. Let's be honest, as much as I was on a serious time crunch on the apartment hunt, talking with Malcolm seemed to ease my stress about it. He knew the right things to say to calm me down, including suggesting I play on my swing-set-jungle-gym-apparatus in the backyard. Perfect guy? Without a doubt.

My parents thought they were being supportive of my moving out by taking the liberty of packing up my stuff for me. I could literally be sucked into my computer: actually, busy searching for apartment listings, and my mother would saunter in my room with a cardboard box or two and just start tossing things on my bookshelves into her organized system. It was what my mother did for a living; she couldn't help it. Our house always looked like the inside of The Container Store. There were storage bins and customized drawers set up all over in the most tasteful way – if storage bins and customized drawers could be considered tasteful. Either way, my mom was the one to make that happen. She had been known to call her label maker her best friend. This was not the run of the mill label maker. No. My mother invested in an industrial strength, highest quality label maker. She called it Max. It was forever in her purses and handbags. She rarely went anywhere without Max. This relationship was almost cruel. Before I started at college, I was filling out all the paperwork for dorm living. However, my mom seemed more excited about organizing my future dorm room than she was about me actually living in it. So I nipped that potential issue in the bud and commuted for four years. At the time, it felt less torturous to live at home during my college years. Oh, how I was wrong about that. My mother and I would constantly fight over the state of and lack of organization in my bedroom. My room was the one dream project for my mom that I refused to let happen. One day, I went out to lunch with Bethany and when I came back, my room had labels all over it! There were labels on everything. There was a label on my closet door. There was a label on my lamp. There was even a label on my hairbrush! Did she really think I couldn't identify the things in my room? It was not a Spanish class in school where they have you identify the objects in a room. Like, garbage, *basura*! That's exactly where all those labels went.

I was never a big fan of my mother's organizational obsession and an overbearing prank like that didn't help our relationship. We would argue about the dumbest stuff and my dad would just sigh and act as referee in the event that things got a little too heated. Oftentimes, he would sit us both down on opposite sides of the dining room table as if he were sending the boxers to their own corners of the ring.

"There will be no raising of voices," my dad would say during the mother-daughter battle throw downs. "I don't want to hear any swearing. I don't want to see anybody give anybody else the stink-eye, Josefina."

"Why is that one directed at me?" I'd admittedly raise my voice and get out of my chair.

Then, my dad would give me that no nonsense look that said it all: Calm down, sit down, and behave yourself. Or else.

I never wanted to know what the "or else" was, so I would usually just slump back in my chair with my arms crossed and sulk with a stink-eye ready.

Perhaps this wasn't the most mature way for me to handle a disagreement. However, it was my way of handling a disagreement.

I never claimed to be mature. A budding adult, yes. Mature, probably not. I wondered how I would handle a disagreement with a roommate. It was inevitable. I hoped I wouldn't blow my cover in the event of an argument. No one could know that I was really five years old at heart -- except everyone who already knew that I was really five years old at heart.

I was aware that I needed to grow up. My parents kept telling me so. I was also aware that my internship was starting in a month and I had no leads on apartments or roommates. The logical thing I thought to do was go outside to pay a visit to my swing-set-jungle-gym-apparatus for a while. I always thought better on that thing. My mind was always clearer and my hopes higher. The drawback was there was no Internet connection while playing on the swing-set-jungle-gym apparatus. Swinging with a laptop in one hand and the other hand holding onto the chain wasn't a potential situation that could occur in the owner's manual. It was a bad idea. But I had a better idea. I found out that I could, in fact, get Internet access while still in the backyard. So of course I brought my computer outside and continued searching for a new place to live in the shade with my old friend.

After I essentially melted into a puddle on the grass, I had that moment. It was the moment that happens after one of the thousands of apartments I had clicked through actually caught my eye. It was a two-bedroom that didn't look half bad. There are some stinker places online. Old, gross tile in kitchens, stained carpet that resembled a crime scene I saw on TV, windows with tape covering the cracks on them, moldy bedroom walls, among other even more less-than-desirable and questionable qualities were described as places "with potential, "lots of sunlight," and my personal favorite, "beautiful hardwood floors." Ha! They can try to pull a fast one on me, but I could see through the deceiving language. You can't mess with an Ivy League graduate! Despite my slight boost in confidence, reality struck me as though I had tried to run through a brick wall and failed. I could find a fantastic apartment, but I couldn't afford it without a roommate. Crap. Back to the drawing board.

I called all of my friends -- well, Bethany and Malcolm -- to see if anyone they knew needed a roommate in New York City and if they needed that roommate ASAP. Bethany was kind of useless. She kept gabbing on about some guy she met at work, but how it wasn't weird because he was a temp and didn't actually work at her job, so she could totally date him. And also something about how she's getting cankles. I told her I had to go because my mom was calling me into the house. So I lied to my best friend and I knew she knew I was lying to her, too. I just had really important things to figure out and I couldn't spend an hour (or two) talking about cankles. I would catch up with her later.

Next on the (very short) list was Malcolm. I was pretty crazy about him, but I didn't want to sound like a crazy person on the phone and start gabbing on about my best friend's cankles. Aside from being awkward, I had a feeling that kind of conversation material would probably scare Malcolm away. I was this close to writing his name with pink swirls and hearts around it in a sparkly notebook like I did with Eric Sanders in the second grade. When my best friend at the time squealed to the entire class that I had a crush on Eric, everyone laughed at me. They didn't let it go until seventh grade when they suddenly found more interesting things to fixate on. In second grade, I had caterpillar eyebrows, purple glasses, a very unfortunate haircut, and I also toted around an orange, stuffed monster doll with me. The way I saw it, why would someone pick on the girl with a monster? Boy, was I wrong. That's partly the reason why I worked so hard to finish high school early. It also sort of explains why I didn't have any close high school friends to speak of. My yearbook had maybe seven signatures. Four of those were from my teachers. Despite my seemingly lonely school years, I turned to books and my imagination to entertain my active mind. When I went to college, things really did get better. There were other offbeat, smart kids just like me and it was totally acceptable. I had found my place in the world for four years. However, I was preparing myself for the transition of my new place in the world for an indeterminate amount of time. It was proving to be much more difficult than I had anticipated.

"Hi, Malcolm," I practiced my phone tone with my right hand in a sort of phone shape that didn't resemble anything close to what a phone actually looks like.

"Hey, Malcolm," I continued rehearsing my greeting.

"How's it shakin', Malcolm?" I shook my head. *No. That won't work. Shakin'? Really? That's a great way to embarrass yourself. Try again.*

This time I tried a sexy voice just for kicks. "Hey, Malcolm. How are things in the big city?" *Epic fail. You are clearly incapable of doing a sexy voice. Be cute. You're good at being cute. It's part of your charm.*

Sadly, I went through that whole preparation process before I ever called anyone on the phone. It was time for some change. So I decided to put on my big girl pants and pick up my real phone and dial Malcolm's number. There was no reason to be nervous. Of course, I started talking myself through the greeting just as he answered the phone.

"Hi, Josefina," he said sweetly.

"Oh, hi, Malcolm," I said in my cutest phone tone voice.

"What's going on?"

"Well," I paused because I realized I hadn't practiced that part of the conversation. "Well, I've been looking for apartments online and now I'm calling everyone I know to see if they know of anyone looking for a roommate in New York. Turns out I don't know a whole lot of people. Any suggestions?" And I exhaled.

"Actually, one of my roommates has a girlfriend who's starting law school somewhere in the city and needs a roommate to live with while she's studying." *Law school! That would have been a good idea...* "He just told me, like, yesterday. She's usually here all the time anyway."

"That sounds like a great idea!"

"I can get her e-mail for you and you can maybe meet up and look at some places together."

"That would be so great. This is going to be great."

I said the word "great" three times in less than a minute. What happened to my vocabulary? I guess it went to mush when Malcolm came into my life. I accepted the sacrifice, but I had to recover from that momentary loss of vocabulary.

"Awesome!" Official epic fail on my part.

Despite making an intellectual fool of myself on the phone with Malcolm, I had a promising lead on a potential roommate. I honestly didn't care who she was, which law school she was going to be attending, if she was messy or neat, or even had a cat. All that mattered to me was that she could pay rent and that we could move into an apartment in the city ASAP.

I sent ReginaSantoro23@email.com a message about an hour after I got off the phone with Malcolm. I said:

> Hi Regina,
>
> You don't know me, but my name is Josefina Ruiz. Your boyfriend's roommate gave me your information. He said you were looking for a roommate for when you start law school in NYC in the fall. Congrats on getting into law school! Anyway, I'm looking for a roommate to live with in NYC before the end of August. So since we're both looking for the same thing on a similar time schedule, I thought maybe we could meet up this weekend and start looking at apartments in the city. Would you be interested in that? My number is 201-555-5525. Let me know your availability. I hope to hear from you really soon.
>
> Thanks!
> Josefina Ruiz

It wasn't my best writing, but considering the day was full of brain farts, I was glad to send out something to this complete stranger that made some sense. I really wanted it to work. I needed it to work. I knew virtually nothing about Regina. I was nervous about the outcome. Hence, I ran around my backyard and made wishes on all the dandelions that had sprouted in the grass. I totally believed in the power of wishes. One time, knowing that goldfishes don't live long, I wished that the little goldfish I won at the school fair would live a long time, like, ten years. I was 10 at the time. The thing finally croaked soon after I turned 20. Wishes have magical powers if you do them right.

When I didn't hear back from Regina for a few hours after my initial message, I decided to try and relax for the night. I had been so preoccupied with the apartment and roommate search, and whatever one would call whatever Malcolm and I are to each other. I was pretty sure we were *officially* dating, but did that mean he was my boyfriend? I really didn't know how to interpret it. Regardless of the swirling thoughts in my head, I knew I deserved a movie night for myself and I fully intended on doing that. One factor stood in my way: my father. He knew how to hog the TV room like he owned it – which he did. Stretched out in front of the television and sinking into the dark brown leather couch with an oversized bowl of popcorn and a glass of wine beside him, my dad was transfixed on the moving pictures in front of him. He was watching some crime solving show. Since he was already occupying the room I had planned to utilize about five minutes earlier, I decided to join in. Why let his mere presence ruin my relaxing night? I sighed, walked over, and plopped myself down on the super comfy couch beside him.

"Hey, kiddo," my dad attempted to instigate conversation. "How's that apartment search going? At least you know where some money will be coming from. Things will fall into place, *mija.*"

"I have a possibility for roommate, but she hasn't responded to my e-mail yet. I just don't know how I'm going to be able to do everything *before* the end of August. I just don't know," I said with complete blank focus on the television. "What are you watching anyway?"

"It's called *Psychic Detectives*," he said with such pride in his choice of show to get hooked on. "This is actually supposed to be a very important episode."

"Oh?"

"Yeah. It's great. See, that guy is the head detective. He's got a whole agency. His name is Scotty. So Scotty sees all these crimes in this fictitious city; it's his job to solve them." he nodded at me as if to: a) see if I was paying attention, and b) try and get me as enthusiastic about this show as he was. "But sometimes he needs to get help solving these crimes. So he calls on this psychic medium. Hence *Psychic Detectives*. Oh! There she is. She's sensing the spirits in the room."

"Uh huh," I said as a nonbeliever.

"It's just about how sometimes you need help from people to figure things out."

"Well, I got some help from my friend Malcolm," I said defensively, taking the show's premise as a personal attack. "His roommate's sister needs a roommate in the city around the same time as me so he thought it would be a good match."

"I see," my dad said repeatedly like he knew something I didn't. I always hated when he did that.

"What is there to see?"

"This *friend* Malcolm, you say, does he live and work in New York?"

"Yes. Actually, his job is really close to my internship. It took me forever to get there and find it that one time, but that's beside –"

"Okay. So he wants you to be closer to him."

"What are you talking about?" I deflected by crossing my arms across my chest.

"Hey. I was not born yesterday, Josefina. You can see that through the wrinkles on my face," he said, oddly pointing to different spots on his face. "This *friend* Malcolm likes you as more than a friend I think."

I brightened up immediately. "Really? You think so?"

He chuckled. "Yes. I do think that. You went to the city with him last weekend, no?" To which I nodded emphatically.

"I am going to remind you, as your father – not that you don't already know this – *cuidate el corazón*. Be careful with your heart. I may not always be here to help you put it back together."

For a moment there, I just looked at my dad with examining eyes trying to figure out what he meant by that. Then, I remembered the fact that he was notorious with his cryptic messages. He thought he was being insightful and wise, but he was really just frustrating when he did that. I was no detective. I was no psychic medium. But I did learn from that conversation that sometimes you really do need help from others to solve the mystery and sometimes you just need someone to share a thoughtful moment with. I was starting to realize that I was fortunate enough to have my dad in my life to give me some decent fatherly advice.

I watched maybe five more minutes of the *Psychic Detectives* show with my dad until my phone buzzed with its possibly defective vibration mode. I thought, *This must be Regina! Maybe not all is lost!* And then I ran to my bedroom, practicing my phone tone voices before finally answering the call.

"Hello?" I said in my introductory phone tone voice. It sounded like me, only phony and more sophisticated simultaneously.

"Is this Josefina Ruiz? This is Regina Santoro," she introduced herself with a dialect that was unfamiliar to me initially. Her voice was super perky, sort of squeaky, and borderline obnoxious. It reminded me of that stereotype people have of Long Island residents, but I didn't want to make judgments too early – not that I had anything against Long Islanders, if that is what you call them.

"Yes! I'm Josefina. It's nice meeting, er, talking to you – on the phone –." I got that out with my usual awkward voice with an uncomfortable laugh to top it off. It seemed to get worse as the conversation continued. Regina kept throwing questions at me that I had no answers to. I clearly didn't know how to manage this proposed arrangement. I needed help. Where was that psychic medium when I really needed her?

This girl was quite a talker, though. My immediate thought was, *How does her boyfriend handle being around her for long stretches of time?* Regina sure knew how to monopolize a conversation.

"I was so thrilled that I was accepted to law school, you know? And especially Columbia University Law School! I'm just a girl from Long Island. My mind was blown. Just, like, *BOOM!*" She burst into a squeaky, obnoxious laugh. "My boyfriend, Roy, do you know him? Well, he went to community college and there's really nothing wrong with that, I just think people should strive for higher accomplishments, you know? Up and up and up, right?" Insert squeaky, obnoxious laugh here, too. "But seriously, down to business –"

"Yes. Can we talk about that?" I attempted to bring the conversation back to the main topic. I had a feeling she wouldn't do so well with the Socratic Method. "Is there a certain neighborhood you like in the city? And how much are you willing to spend on rent?"

"Oh, I love the Village! It's so cute, you know?"

As she was gabbing on, I pulled up a map of Manhattan on my computer with all the big neighborhoods color-coded.

"Regina, when you say you love the Village, which 'Village' are you referring to?"

And then another squeaky, obnoxious laugh. "The West Village, of course!"

"Okay. I just didn't –"

"Oh, yes. The West Village is the best! I hear it's pretty expensive to live there, though. I also like the Upper East Side. But that wouldn't be very practical for me considering I'm going to Columbia Law School! Woot! Woot!"

I honestly didn't know what to make of her. She was capable of being serious, but then she would pop out of that and start woot wooting. I did guess right about the Long Island thing, though. That was pretty impressive for my lack of experience with New York accents. Woot. Woot. Maybe there was more to her that I couldn't get from speaking on the phone. We decided to meet the next day in Manhattan to further discuss what we were trying to nail down the night before. We also agreed to bring as many apartment listings as we could find that fit in our profile of budget and location.

We were to meet in the center of Penn Station since her train from Long Island was arriving there 10 minutes after mine. I was prepared to travel through every inch of the city. I wore a royal blue tank top, green shorts, and sneakers so hopefully my feet wouldn't give way half-way through the day. I didn't know what she looked like. All I knew was her perky, squeaky, obnoxious voice, which was amplified by the phone mechanism. So I was searching a busy train station terminal for some person who might match the voice. It was not going to be easy when the only people who really spoke were those commuters conversing on their phones. Sifting through the crowds wasn't easy. I mastered the bob and weave technique of getting from point A to point B in a metropolitan train station. Regina must have seen my skills or my awkward searching. She followed me until I stopped for a moment somewhere along the line.

"Josefina?" Regina asked as she tapped on my shoulder to catch my attention.

I turned around, startled by her unexpected presence behind me. "Regina?"

"Yes! Oh, sweetie. Were you lost looking for me in Penn Station?"

"I wasn't lost," I said defensively.

"Well, you looked kinda lost. It's okay. We found each other!" she squealed as she hugged me.

"Uh huh," I mumbled.

So we headed somewhere to review our apartment picks. Regina had a place in mind. It was further downtown on Seventh Avenue. She said she loved taking all her friends there when they were in the city. I guess she hoped we would become friends. We arrived at the Friends Cafe on 20th Street and Seventh Avenue. It was appropriately named. However, I couldn't tell if it was named for actual friends or after the TV show. Walking in, it smelled kind of musty. Regina motioned for me take a seat on one of the couches. When I sat down, dust erupted from the cushion. Immediately, I began sneezing hysterically.

"Isn't this place great?" Regina said, completely ignoring my sneezing attack.

"Yeah, it's great." I said as I wiped my nose. "So which listings did you bring? If we can, I think we should see as many as we can today."

"I agree. The market for real estate in this city is *crazy*, you know?" She took out her tablet and started tapping around at the screen. "I found a few in the West Village and on the Upper West Side, near the Columbia campus. Gotta have that convenience, you know?"

"Yeah, I know," I said as she pushed the tablet on the super small table toward me. "I was actually considering a place somewhere on the West Side. My internship is on West 24th Street and Sixth Avenue, so if I can be in a place on the West Side, I think that would be really convenient for me."

I was so impressed at how I talked the talk about neighborhoods in New York City like I actually knew the city and had actually been to the places we were discussing. I'd be a New Yorker in no time.

Regina and I journeyed throughout the entire West Side of Manhattan in search of the perfect apartment. Apparently, that didn't exist in the city with our meager budget. My parents said they would pitch in so I could pay for the first month's rent and security deposit until my regular paychecks from J.A.M. came in. That said, they capped the budget at 750 dollars per month, which was a reasonable amount considering I wanted to be able to buy things like, well, food. And I heard it was important to pay bills or else live in the dark. So I needed to have money left over. We decided to split the rent equally so our combined maximum budget would be $1,500, which in this city would barely get you as far as a very small studio apartment. As disappointing as that reality was, we needed to press on. We both had deadlines and that was causing tension and stress. None of the apartments we looked at were even close to satisfying our needs as roommates and tenants. After the 14th apartment we looked at, a distressing time crunch set in. We had one more listing left on our list.

"Lucky number 15!" I said with my last drop of enthusiasm.

This one was on Clinton Street. I didn't have any idea where that was. For all I knew, it was in The Bronx. I could figure out numbered streets. That was no problem. Deciphering the reasoning behind the order of named streets in Manhattan was something that years at an Ivy League university couldn't prepare me for. Luckily, Regina had her smart phone with her so she could look up the map and locate this last apartment. If only I had upgraded my dumb phone for something that actually had some useful artificial intelligence. We rested in the shade on a stoop somewhere near West 40th Street. All the streets started blending together. I couldn't remember where we had basically collapsed from exhaustion.

"Well, it's in the Village," she said, vigorously tapping her phone. "Sort of."

"That's where you wanted to go, right?" I asked naively.

"It's actually in the Lower East Side."

"Oh," I cowered. "Well, it's the last place on our list. It might be worth checking out."

Regina exhaled an exasperated sigh. "Yeah. I guess we could," she said, taking a swig from her water bottle.

It was a hot day – just like the day I explored Manhattan with Malcolm. In fact, it was so hot that Regina's makeup had started melting off her face within an hour of trekking through the streets of New York. I wasn't wearing any makeup besides waterproof mascara. It was simply impractical to wear anything that could potentially smudge.

"It's kinda far from here, though," Regina continued. "We would have to take the subway, you know?"

"Do you know which one to take?" I asked. "I'm not really familiar with the subway system."

She shot me a look and motioned for me to get up off the stoop I had turned into a cooling off area and follow her. Clearly, the heat did not agree with her attitude or her hair. We took the F train down to Delancey Street. Walking up the subway steps to the street was grueling, but we both made it up to the surface alive. Then, we found a spot in the shade under an awning that was above a closed storefront as we waited for Regina's phone to recognize where we were and direct us to the apartment. As I waited, all I could do was stand there and observe the environment around me. The rhythm of the streets were completely different from anything I had ever been immersed in. The people and buildings were more vibrant than in any neighborhood we had explored on the West Side of Manhattan. I could even hear some salsa music playing somewhere on the street like a built-in soundtrack. It reminded me of my grandmother's house in Rincón, Puerto Rico. She always loved to dance to salsa music even when her knees wouldn't quite cooperate. I was named after Abuelita Josefina. She was short in stature, but she was one of the most intelligent people I had ever known. An expert domino player, she taught me all the mathematical tricks and strategies to the game. Because of her, I was always a hit at family gatherings, scoring over the older men who would assume I wasn't skilled at the game of numbered tiles. Boo-yah! I was always the unexpected winner. Abuelita Josefina's health had started to deteriorate, but she was still getting on. She wasn't as strong as she used to be, but she still had her wits about her. I was rusty, but I really wished I could go to Puerto Rico to play dominoes against her and brush up on my Spanish.

"It's this way," Regina popped my thought bubble and hurried on to the next turning point. "I think it's a left at the next block." She continued talking, but I didn't really listen to her. I was too engrossed in this new world that surrounded me. I simply followed her and the GPS so I wouldn't get completely lost. "God, I hate these named streets," Regina complained in her more-and-more-obnoxious-every-second-how-am-I-going-to-stand-living-with-her voice.

We walked down a quiet block (compared to the bustle of Delancey Street). The buildings looked old. The sidewalk was cracked. The storefront below the building we were looking at was closed. Things didn't look promising. However, there was a cute comic book shop next door to the building called Clinton Street Comics. It wasn't a very clever name for a comic book shop, but at least it showed signs of life.

"We're here," my future roommate said.

"The listing says it's on the third floor and to ring the bell when we get there," I said as I read the instructions from the piece of paper I had been clutching in my sweaty palm.

This was our last shot of the day to find an apartment worth living in. The clock was ticking and I felt like I was going in slow motion, but that my universe was traveling at a speed I couldn't maintain. So I went up to the door and pushed the buzzer button for apartment 3D. We were buzzed into the building within seconds and immediately took a good look around the space. It didn't look as run-down as I thought it would from the outside. The stairs had a red, patterned carpet runner. It was a little worn, but not terrible. The walls looked like they were painted sort of recently; I couldn't really tell. I'm not a paint specialist, but the walls were a shade of beige; let's call it taupe. We hiked up the three flights of stairs to meet the building manager at the landing. He looked sharp in a grey suit, white shirt, and blue striped tie. Every garment looked precisely pressed and his shoes were impeccably polished. His hair was slicked back to perfection. I almost expected him to pull out a pocket watch. However, he was surprisingly young for a building manager. My guess was that he was around 30 or so.

"Hello and welcome to 16 Clinton Street," he greeted us with radio announcer-type voice. "I'm Barnaby Peabody, building manager. You can call me Barnaby. Are you girls here to see the apartment?"

Regina wasted no time and jumped right in saying, "Hi, Barnaby. My name is Regina Santoro." She looked at him – no – *gazed* at him with a twinkle in her eye. Forget about Roy, she found a newer, (seemingly) more mature male prospect to flirt with. At this point, she was practically drooling on the floor as he readjusted his perfectly coiffed hair. I wondered how much hair spray he needed to get that look just right.

"I'm Josefina Ruiz," I introduced myself to break Regina out of her fantasy land so we could see the apartment.

"This is a two-bedroom, one bath apartment, okay?" Barnaby said matter of factly as if to say, *What you see is what you get.* I immediately expected the worst as he led us down the end of the hall.

My fingers and toes were all crossed as I wished to whomever grants wishes these days. I even closed my eyes when he unlocked the forest green-colored door. I liked green. I could work with green. I opened my eyes just as Barnaby swung open the door. Light poured in from the tall windows along the left-side wall. Regina and I stepped in. My first instinct was to find out what the view was from the windows. I bee-lined it to the middle of the living room's three windows. There was another apartment building directly across, but luckily, it was on the other side of the street. A cute little garden was situated below us. I must have spent far too much time admiring the view from the wonderful, sunshine-filled windows before me because Regina started calling my name, loudly.

"Josefina, I don't know what you're looking at over there, but there is more to this apartment than those windows." She sounded like my mother and I didn't like it.

I turned away from the windows as though it were a bittersweet goodbye, crossed the jumbo-sized living room space, and continued to look at what the rest of the apartment had to offer. I genuinely thought the kitchen was nice. Regina thought the opposite. She said the cabinets looked too 1983 or something like that. I wasn't really listening. In my opinion, the retro cabinets looked like '83 chic – in her mind, I was clearly wrong. She rolled her eyes at me and shook her head. Next, were the bedrooms; I thought they were generally the same size. Both bedrooms had one large window each and had the same dimensions in their layout. I checked the detail with Regina's new boyfriend prospect, Barnaby Peabody. Then, we looked at the bathroom. Regina was completely disgusted by the mint green and black tiles that lined the walls. As a lover of the color green, I didn't mind the tile at all. It was well maintained and I thought it gave the place some more retro character.

"You just said the 1980s kitchen cabinets added some 'retro character,'" Regina jabbed and returned to judge the rest of the apartment.

I seriously considered looking for a new roommate. There was only so much I could take of her attitude. She started out all, 'I'm going to law school! Woot! Woot!' Somehow she had turned into MegaBitch, the superhero whose comic book series was abruptly discontinued and now she has an evil plot to take over the world. Surely, Clinton Street Comics would carry rare copies of it. But in all seriousness, she was getting excruciatingly annoying.

One thing that I noticed was that there was already air conditioning in the apartment. I wasn't sweating uncontrollably. It was glorious.

"Hey, Barnaby," I approached him as he was engrossed in playing some game on his phone. He was slightly startled. It didn't phase me. "Is there air conditioning in the building?"

"Yep," he confirmed. "It's included in the rent. That, hot water, and heat are included."

That's when I put on my serious game face on. It's one thing I definitely learned from playing dominoes with Abuelita Josefina.

"Okay, Barnaby. You say central air, heat, *and* hot water are included in the rent?" I interrogated.

He nodded to answer my question.

"The listing said the rent price was to be determined. I'll take it for one thousand."

"Josefina! What are you saying!" Regina piped in and I shushed her to be quiet. I was playing hardball.

"I can't give it to you for a thousand," Barnaby layed his next domino. "How about we say 1,700?"

In my mind, I knew that was a *steal* for a decent two-bedroom apartment in Manhattan, but I was already in the game and I was playing to win. Also, $1,700 was still above our combined budget. I needed to negotiate further.

"One thousand, one hundred, flat," I made my next move.

"What are you doing, Josefina! I don't even know if I like this place, you know?" Regina loudly chimed in. I simply waved my hand and her as if to so say, *SHUT UP!*

Barnaby squinted at me for a long minute considering how to counter my offer. I had read in a book I found in the library that it was fair game to negotiate rent prices. So there I was, negotiating.

"Okay. I'll give you the apartment for $1,500," Barnaby stated, putting down another domino, but knowing he didn't have the right tiles to win. "You do realize $1,500 is dirt cheap for *any* apartment in this city, right?"

"I know. I also know you're going to let us move into this apartment for less than that," I said like an old pro at a car dealership.

"Oh, yeah?" he tried to call my bluff.

"Yeah."

Regina stood next to me for that strength in numbers thing. It wasn't like he was doing something bad. I just wanted a better price and I wasn't going to settle. If we were going to take this apartment – though Regina already told me she hates the mint green tiles more than she hates the Boogey Man – we were going to live there at our price.

"$1,450," I said very deliberately, setting down my final domino. I don't know where I was getting all the *coraje*, courage, but I was enjoying playing the game.

Barnaby stood there, leaning against the door like he was the ultimate cool dude. I could tell he was crunching numbers. Then, he extended his hand out to me.

"Okay, lady. You've got yourself a deal. $1,450 per month with air conditioning, heat, *and* hot water included," Barnaby admitted defeat. "It's rent destabilized anyway."

Hearing him say that was like winning the whole dominoes game with a *capicu* or palindrome tile and finishing the game on both ends.

I shook his hand firmly. "Where do we sign?"

I looked at Regina who was overjoyed over the amazing deal I just negotiated for us *and* that she would get to see Barnaby Peabody on a regular basis around the building. She made me promise that I wouldn't tell Roy *or* Malcolm about her little crush. I was still in shock over how well I managed to keep that poker face on. Usually, after a while I break out laughing. Maybe the ability to be serious about something for more than two minutes was part of growing up. Was that the next stage of growing up?

CHAPTER TEN

"What you leave behind is not what is engraved in stone monuments, but what is woven into the lives of others." – Pericles

"Did you want to bring this, Josie?" Bethany asked skeptically, holding a lamp with a base covered in painted macaroni pieces.

Bethany volunteered to help me pack up my life in Bellcastle, New Jersey to begin a new life in New York City. I begrudgingly allowed my mother to help in the process.

"Oh, I remember when Josefina made that!" my mother reminisced. "She was in kindergarten. So cute. You loved to have your hair in these pigtails –"

"Okay. I was a cute kid who loved macaroni," I interrupted.

"You *still* love macaroni!" my mother quipped. "You had macaroni and cheese for lunch yesterday."

I paused for a moment. "Okay. Fine. I still like macaroni."

They both giggled at my not-so-secret confession.

"At least you don't drink from those little juice boxes," Bethany said.

"And what if I do?" I responded with six year old sass.

My mother mediated, "Ay, Josefina. Grow up, please, *por favor.*"

Those words, "grow up," stung like a papercut, peroxide, and bee sting simultaneously. I was offended not only because I was venturing into this very grown up stage of my life called moving out on my own,

102

but because she was just supposed to be helping me pack. We had an agreement prior to packing day that my mother would engage in conversation as little as possible and simply help me put things in boxes in an organized fashion. I decided that if she wanted me to grow up, I would take on a persona she could comprehend: Miss Boss Lady.

"Mom, can you put that label maker to good use, please," I ordered.

"*¡Oye! ¿Qué te pasa?* What's the matter?" my mother barked at me. When she broke out the Spanish, I knew I was in trouble.

"I said 'please'" I responded meekly.

"Josefina Susana Ruiz. I do not appreciate this attitude."

"Sorry," I cowered as she full-named me.

"I know you are becoming all grown up, moving to New York City, but being grown up does not give you permission to treat me or anyone else with this temper of yours. I will not accept it from you," my mother said with authority. "I didn't raise you to be that way either. You know better."

She stood there, staring me down, waiting for a true apology that was sincere rather than out of fear. I looked over at Bethany, who had taken a seat in my desk chair, out of the crossfire. Truthfully, I really didn't want to fight with my mother in that moment. I just wanted to get all of my stuff into boxes so I could put them in a truck and settle into my life as an adult. I really hated that my mother was treating me like a 10 year old with an attitude problem. My mother's comment was insulting. Whether she intended to insult me or not was superfluous. I was hurt and I needed more than a cartoon character on a bandage to fix it.

"Mother," I said calmly. "I think I need some space. I'm going to leave my room for a few minutes. I'll be back when I'm able to continue packing." How's that for mature and grown up? My mother stood there shocked and speechless. "Bethany?" I summoned my best friend to follow me as I left my bedroom.

Bethany chased me downstairs and outside as I hurried to my swing-set-jungle-gym-apparatus. I took a seat at the swings and took off as she trailed. My eyes began welling up with tears. I didn't notice Bethany; I almost hit her in the face with my feet while swinging.

"Whoa!" Bethany called out as she maneuvered away from the danger zone and into the seat beside mine. "Josie, what is going on with you? I have never seen you act that way with anyone, especially your mom."

I wiped a tear out of my right eye and said, "I don't know." I kept on swinging. "I think I just need to clear my head. Everything is changing so quickly. Like, first, I *didn't* get the internship. Then, I did, which meant I needed to move to New York, which is scary enough to begin with. So next, I had to find an apartment *and* a roommate, which aren't so easy to come by. I'm tired and I'm scared and I know I have no idea what I'm doing." I wiped a few more tears of out my eyes.

"It's okay to be scared about that," Bethany said. "Look, I didn't know exactly what I was doing when I moved into my apartment in Morristown to be closer to work. I think it's scary for everyone. You'll figure it out. And we won't be so far away. I will need to see that new, grown up city apartment of yours."

My swinging pace slowed down. I wiped a few more tears from my face and tried to gather my words. "I'm just really overwhelmed and my mom telling me to grow up isn't helping my anxiety about actually growing up."

"You're a forever-kid, Josie."

"Yeah," I said. "It's just that nothing in my forever-kid world has prepared me for any of this."

"I don't think anything really will. That's the fun of it. It's like reading a series of epic novels and you won't know how it ends until the final book comes out," Bethany explained.

"I guess," I said.

"Besides, everyone has to move on from being a forever-kid sometime," Bethany interjected. "Unless you're, like, Peter Pan."

Looking around at my backyard filled with childhood memories, it suddenly dawned on me that I wanted to be a forever-kid. I aspired to be a forever-kid. It was my perfect occupation. Josefina Ruiz: forever-kid. I could print up business cards. That's what I wanted to be when I grew up. Being an adult seemed overrated. Adulthood comes with so many responsibilities, like paying the rent and paying the electricity bill. It seemed as though being an adult included a lot of paying for expensive things. Being a kid was like living the dream to me. I didn't really want to grow up. I wasn't in a rush. I just wanted to play on my swing-set-jungle-gym-apparatus to my heart's content. If I could do that every day (and get paid for it), I would be one happy camper. Alas, that wasn't my reality and I did need to grow up. Maybe my mother was right.

Bethany decided to go home for the night. I returned to my bedroom, where my mom sat on my bed, holding a picture frame in her hands.

"Mom," I said upon walking across the threshold.

My mother looked up, "Yes, Josefina. What is it?"

"Are you crying?" I asked just as she stealthily wiped a tear from her eyes.

"Would that be so surprising?"

"No. I just don't know what you're crying about."

"While you were downstairs, I continued packing some of your things. I found this frame with a picture of you and me when we went to the Central Park Zoo. You must have been five years old," my mother reminisced.

"We went to Central Park when I was a kid? Why don't I remember that?"

"You were very young. *Mira*, look, your hair was in those pigtails you loved so much," she passed the frame to me as I sat beside her at the foot of my bed. My mother wiped away another tear.

"Mom, why are you so sad? I'm not moving that far away."

"I'm just thinking about how different things will be without you here all the time. The house will be quieter. I won't have anyone to make pancakes for," she said. "But, I see you blossoming into a beautiful young woman and I am so proud. Maybe I don't tell you that enough, but I am so proud of you, Josefina."

I gave my mom a big hug and didn't want to let go. I knew that if I let go, it would mean that a chapter in my life was ending. It was like a chapter in a book that I had read a hundred times. I knew how it was supposed to go. No surprises. No rude awakenings. No unexpected life changes. I longed for a completely predictable life. That was the impossible dream. It was also just another fantasy that I would have to pack away into a box.

My dad rented a U-Haul to transport my stuff from my real home to my new home. It wasn't as though I had a whole lot of stuff to bring with me; I was leaving most of the odds and ends that resembled my childhood with my parents. I knew I wasn't going to be able to fit a whole lot of furniture in my new room, so I purposefully didn't pack much besides my bed frame, mattress, a nightstand, and a lamp. The remaining boxes were filled with my clothes and books.

I was still in disbelief. The fact that I was really moving hadn't hit me yet. I said goodbye to everything in the house as though I would never return and this was the last time I would see any of the things that lived in my house. I stood in the doorway to my room, took a good look around, and closed the door. After I walked downstairs and strolled through the kitchen, I caught a glance of my swing-set-jungle-gym-apparatus. I knew there wasn't enough time for me to play on it before we had to leave, which only pulled at my heartstrings. I mouthed a "goodbye, old friend" to it through the screen door window and continued saying my farewell to my childhood home. I even gave my old car a proper goodbye by sitting in it and pillaging it for anything I wanted to keep from it, which was, well, not a lot. I found a pen with a fluffy top and a package of post-its in the glove compartment. That was as much as I could salvage. My dad said he was going to get rid of it after I left. After I was done bidding farewell to my car, I rejoined my moving crew A.K.A. my parents and Bethany. Malcolm said he would meet us at the apartment. We loaded ourselves into my dad's SUV with the U-Haul attached to the back.

"Did you make sure you have everything, Josefina?" my dad asked from the driver's seat prior to pulling away from the curb.

I gazed out the window at the house that would no longer be my home. "What?" I snapped out of my trance. "Oh, yeah. I got everything, dad. We can go."

And with that, we pulled away from the curb. The ride into the city was quiet. I could tell Bethany wanted to ask me questions about Malcolm since she would be meeting him for the first time. However, gabbing on about Malcolm in front of my parents in the confines of a moving vehicle was not exactly the wisest thing to do. She texted me instead:

BETHANY: Is Malcolm bringing any cute friends with him? ;)

ME: I don't know. His roommate Roy will be there but he's taken. That's all I know.

BETHANY: You should tell him to bring some hot friends to help out.

ME: Haha. I think I'll have plenty of help. I don't have that much stuff.

BETHANY: Yeah. But he doesn't know that. Haha.

Eventually, we emerged from the Holland Tunnel and made our way to 16 Clinton Street, New York, NY. It dawned on me that I didn't know my new zip code. I needed to look that up.

"This is it," I called out in excitement when we turned onto the street that would be my residence.

"There's a comic book shop on this block. That's cool," Bethany said. "If you're into that kind of thing."

I shot her a disapproving look to which she mouthed a 'Sorry.' Then, I saw Malcolm making his way down the block. Luckily, there was a parking spot available in front of the building to make the moving process easier. Upon my father applying the parking brake on his car, I opened the door and hopped out to call out to Malcolm. Bethany took her time getting out of the back seat. She ended up leaning against the car with her arms crossed as my parents opened up the trunk and U-Haul, and I spent time greeting Malcolm with a hug.

"Aren't you going to introduce me, Josefina?" Bethany asked as she tried to look cool with her arms crossed standing next to my dad's SUV. Mind you, she was also wearing an old, oversized T-shirt she got at freshman orientation. It looked like she was wearing an orange and black sack that was too long to be called a T-shirt and too short to be considered a dress. It was not the best I've seen her look.

"Malcolm, this is my best friend, Bethany," I introduced. "She's like my sister."

Bethany held out her hand for Malcolm to shake. "Nice to meet you. Are you bringing any friends with you?"

He was stunned and speechless at Bethany's rather forthright question. "Um–" he muttered.

"You know, to help you haul all of Josefina's stuff upstairs?" Bethany winked at me. I rolled my eyes.

"What she means, Malcolm, is she wants to know if you have any cute friends for her to date," I interjected.

"Josefina!" Bethany reacted with disappointment. "You totally blew my cover. Nice going. All I wanted was a date." She returned to crossing her arms and leaning against the car.

"So this is your BFF Bethany," Malcolm said. "I may have a buddy who might be interested."

Bethany perked up, went over to Malcolm, and gave him a big hug. I wondered if she had something to drink earlier in the morning because she was acting so strangely. I almost expected her to break out singing a random song, which honestly, would have ruined all her chances at getting a date.

"I like this guy, Josie." Ditto.

My father called out to us so we could help unload my stuff and bring it all upstairs. I introduced Malcolm to both my parents and I was happily surprised at how pleasant they were with him. They were usually big on tough love and checking to see if they really trusted a person. However, in this instance, there was handshaking involved and lots of smiling. Of course, I had no other experience to compare it to, but the meeting of the parents scenes in movies never seemed to go as smoothly as this. It was a topsy-turvy day. My mother insisted that she have a look at the apartment before we bring anything up. So we all took a field trip to the third floor. Barnaby Peabody had already given Regina and I our keys to the building and apartment to make moving in easier considering we were going to be setting up shop the next week. I opened the door with what seemed like a caravan of people behind me in the hallway. The caravan followed me into the living room and instantaneously spread out.

"Look at these windows, Josefina!" my mom commented immediately upon stepping over the threshold. "How nice."

"It's my favorite part of this place." I was glad to hear that someone else was as obsessed with those windows as I was.

My father and Malcolm inspected the kitchen. Together. And they were getting along. Quite well. I didn't know exactly how to deal with that situation so I looked for Bethany. I found her checking out the bathroom.

"You know you have green tile in here, right?" Bethany commented.

"Yes. I like it," I defended the questionable bathroom design. "Don't worry. It's clean. I checked."

"I just don't understand how you can actually like neon green bathroom tile."

"You sound like Regina," I said.

"Oh, yeah. Where is that roommate of yours?" Bethany asked as she inspected every tile on the wall.

I left her to obsess over the green bathroom and went back to the kitchen to find Malcolm.

"Malcolm, have you heard from Roy or Regina today?"

"Roy was still sleeping when I left to come here, so I don't know where he is now. I have no idea about Regina, but I'm assuming she's coming in from Long Island," Malcolm explained.

"Okay," I responded. "I just thought she would be here by now. It's 11 a.m."

"Maybe you should call her," he suggested.

I pulled my phone out of my pocket and dialed Regina. It rang and rang and rang and went to voicemail. I also sent her a text asking what her ETA was. No response.

"*¡Ay, Dios!*" my mother called out from out of my sight line. "Oh my God, Josefina! You have a neon green bathroom." She walked around the corner, looked at me, and pointed to the bathroom door. "Did you know this?"

"Yes. I like it green."

"Why?" she continued to push the subject.

Then, my phone buzzed so I just pointed to it and walked over to the windows I also thought were unique.

"Hi, Regina," I answered.

"Hi, Josefina. We're stuck in terrible traffic going into Manhattan. It's like everyone in Long Island decided to evacuate at the same time or something. I'll be there as soon as I can, once we get out of this awful traffic, you know? Pick whichever room you want, okay? Hopefully I'll be there soon. Gotta go," Regina explained her tardiness and hung up the phone with a click.

I returned to the kitchen, where everyone had congregated.

"Regina's on her way. She's stuck in traffic getting into the city. So let's bring everything up, okay?" I turned toward the door and motioned everyone to follow me. "All right then."

Malcolm and my dad took care of my full size mattress. Bethany and I brought up the bed frame. My mother carried the first box of clothes up the stairs. We were like a well -oiled machine. Eventually, we were down to the last box, which contained my books. I decided to bring it up to my room on my own. It was also the heaviest of all the boxes I had packed of sentimental things from home. I had already read all the books in the box. The prized collection needed a safe place near me. Before I could bring them up, I needed to say goodbye to my parents. I had almost forgotten that from that point on, I wasn't going to be living with them anymore. My brain still hadn't registered that fact. I was too distracted by the move to even think about it. I sent Bethany to discuss possible suitors with Malcolm while I bid farewell to the people who raised me into the person I had become. I was sad to be leaving them, but I was happy to not have to live with my parents anymore.

"We are so proud of you, *mija*," my dad said. "The house is going to be so quiet without you there."

"Dad, it's not like I'm going to be gone forever. I'll still be able to go back home and visit."

"Of course you can," he gave me a hug that felt like it lasted for hours. I could tell he didn't want to let go.

"Okay, Jorge," my mother interrupted. "Is it my turn to say good-bye to our daughter yet?"

"Thanks for everything, dad. I'm going to miss watching 'Psychic Detectives' with you."

"Me too, Josefina. Me too."

I turned to my mother and she enveloped me in her arms. I could tell she was crying, which in turn made me cry. She didn't want to let go either.

"You're going to do great things. I can't wait to see what a successful young lady you will become," she managed to say beyond the tears. "You'll always be my little girl. I love you, *mija.*"

I hugged her tighter. "I love you, too, mom."

Somehow we pulled ourselves apart. My mom wiped some tears from her eyes.

"Don't forget to actually take those things *out* of the boxes, okay?" she nagged like mothers do. "And hang up your clothes. I don't want to hear that you're still living out of boxes three months from now. And remember to call."

"I know, mom. I know."

My parents gave me final hugs and kisses and then, they drove back to Bellcastle, New Jersey with Bethany in tow. She couldn't stay over. Work beckoned her. Malcolm offered to help me put some things away so I wouldn't be living out of boxes three months out. I told him that I was just really tired from the move and that I would text him later on and maybe we could hang out the following day. So I sent him home with one little good night kiss. I wanted to be alone for a while and take in the big event of the day. Finally, I picked up the last box of books that needed to go in my apartment and walked up the stairs to the third floor. It was my new home. Bellcastle would no longer be my home. It would just be the town where my childhood home was rooted. Part of that made me feel liberated and part of it made me extremely sad. It was a lot to get used to in one day. Regina called earlier to say she was going to be coming to the apartment later on that evening to move in. That meant that I would be alone for most of the night, which would only give me more time to sit around and think too much about the future. It felt like the world was moving so fast all the time. I couldn't catch a moment to slow down and absorb everything that was happening around me. Being an only child, I had to learn how to entertain myself. Usually, I would take to my swing-set-jungle-gym-apparatus and use my imagination to think of some world or distant planet I could fly away to. Living in New York City was going to make it really hard to make that happen every time I get bored. I was hard-pressed to find a swing set I was actually allowed to play on in this city.

After getting back to the apartment, I walked over to the bedroom I chose. The bedrooms were just about the same size with one large window each. Regina said I should pick whichever room I wanted. I was glad I had my own room. Living within such close quarters of someone with absolutely no privacy would not work for me. I opened my bedroom door and placed the box of books on top of an already existing pile of boxes. I could have hung up my clothes so they wouldn't just sit in their boxes. I should have done that. Instead, I sat in the middle of my bed, looking toward my one large window that looked toward the street. The street lamp across the way had an inviting glow about it, almost assuring me that I was home. This was where I needed to be. I convinced myself that I was going to be okay. It was a big change that I knew I wouldn't get used to for a while. At least reality was starting to set in, rather than playing pretend in my mind.

CHAPTER ELEVEN

"Courage is knowing what not to fear." – Plato

I stayed in the apartment for a whole day after initially moving in confined within the walls like a prisoner or something. I was a prisoner of my own fear. Although I was getting used to New York City prior to the move, anxiety about exploring the streets alone was intimidating. I was sure to get lost. Carrying a map while wandering through the city seemed like a bad idea despite the major factor that I didn't own a map in the first place.

"You should really get out there, Josefina," Regina encouraged. "It's a beautiful day, you know? OOH! You should try figuring out the subway system or figure out how to get to your new job or you could go buy some groceries for yourself."

I knew she meant well. And she was right. I had been living off a sub sandwich that my dad got for me at some deli down at the corner of the block and granola for the past day. This was now officially day two and I was getting hungry.

Regina continued, "I'm going to pick up my books for my *law school* classes. I start next week, too!"

She said *"law school"* with such a conceited air. It was almost as if she were saying "Look at me! I go to law school! Aren't I special!" Well, la de da de da for her. I was the one who negotiated the rent on the apartment, not the law school student. I was getting cynical. I needed to be outside. So I actually took Regina's advice to heart and headed off to my mint green tiled bathroom to shower and get myself ready for the day. When I finally deemed myself appropriately dressed for my first day as a New York City resident, I marched into the hall, down the stairs, and out the front door into the sun. I immediately put on my sunglasses and decided a direction to walk in. I didn't know if it was the right way or the wrong way. I didn't even know where I was going. But I needed to go somewhere. Anywhere. And eventually find my way back home.

I decided that for my first solo outing, I needed to be tough – or at least look tough. My logic told me that a no nonsense facial expression would deter passersby from messing with me. So I plastered a serious-looking face on the original. My eyebrows were furrowed, and overall, I looked like a lunatic. I checked myself out in an empty, parked car's side view mirror. I was delirious to think some ridiculous face would keep the bad guys away from me. Clearly, I wasn't a scary looking person. I still rocked the tourist look, which instantly made me a target for people trying to sell umbrellas on a sunny day, guys selling cheap handbags from tables on the corners, and generally, any "entrepreneurs." After reaching Delancey Street and walking for a few blocks, I ditched my scary look and traded it in for the Josefina look. I heard it's all the rage in Puerto Rico.

Delancey Street was vibrant and eclectic, and I loved it. There were bodegas on every corner, a plethora of bars and restaurants, and a variety of shops lined the busy street. It fed into the Williamsburg Bridge. I learned that by reading a sign that said "Williamsburg Bridge Ahead." If I ever needed to go to Williamsburg, I would know which bridge to take. However, I wasn't as well versed with the city yet, so I still wasn't exactly sure if Williamsburg was in Brooklyn or Queens. I really needed to buy a map. I found myself enthralled with my surroundings. Something about this neighborhood drew me in. It was as if I was meant to be there.

As I continued to absorb Delancey Street, I approached a subway station for the F train. I decided to take Regina's advice and figure out my route to my brand-spanking-new internship on West 24th Street.

Beautiful days like this can bring memorable adventures. You have to seek out the adventure in your life. I recalled a Philosophy professor mention something wise like that in one of my classes at Princeton.

I wasn't sure where the F train would lead me. All I knew was that I was downtown and Jarvis Advertising and Marketing was uptown on 24th Street. I swiped what was left on my MetroCard and waited in the sweltering dungeon that was the New York City subway platform. After about 15 minutes, an uptown F train arrived. I boarded and rode the air-conditioned train until we arrived on a street that seemed somewhat close to West 24th Street and Sixth Avenue. I figured if I got lost, so be it. I had nowhere else to be. 2nd Avenue passed, followed by the Broadway-Lafayette Street stop, then West 4th Street-Washington Square, and 14th Street. The conductor announced that the next stop would be 23rd Street. Huzzah! What a fluke! I actually got on the right train! I would be a New Yorker soon enough. This was a small victory. Once I emerged at the top of the Mount Everest-like subway stairs, I would still need to navigate myself in the right direction of the J.A.M. offices. Last time I was on 23rd Street and Sixth Avenue, I couldn't figure out which was East or West. I hoped I'd have better luck this time. This particular time, disoriented from the train ride and not knowing where the exits in the tunnel were located, I accidentally stepped on another girl's flip-flop, to which she looked at me with the stink eye. Somehow I wasn't surprised by that reaction. I guess I was already adjusting to that New Yorker attitude.

Something about the intersection of 23rd Street and Sixth Avenue felt familiar. I knew I had seen this pavement and these buildings before. However, somehow, I couldn't figure out where I was and which way to walk. People pushed past me on the street and I retreated to an alcove between storefronts to gather my bearings. My eyes adjusted to the surroundings so I could remember something about that day of my interview and the rain that transpired. Apparently, the rain had washed away most of my memory of the wet, Manhattan streets. All I could remember was the sidewalk. Perhaps keeping my head down to shelter myself from the rain wasn't a good tactic for staying dry. Still, I knew that the J.A.M. offices were located on West 24th Street. Therefore, I needed to find West 24th Street without getting trampled. When the crosswalk sign turned to "Walk," I hurried across Sixth Avenue to the other side of 23rd Street. I walked a few steps up the avenue to see what the next street sign read: West 24th Street. In my mind, I was officially a genius for being able to figure that out.

I stood in front of the building's doors and stared up at the floors above, contemplating my future and what I actually expected from my upcoming days as an intern. The connotation that accompanied the term "intern" wasn't always a positive one. I dreaded the thought of having to fetch coffee for everyone in the office in the morning, at lunchtime, and at the end of the day. The possibility of that idea seeped into my consciousness. I tried to hold onto a more positive outlook. Hopefully, the internship would be meaningful with real job opportunities to look forward to. I would be an intern at J.A.M. for six months, as the paperwork I signed documented. I imagined what it would be like being a working individual. It was a new experience. Honestly, I wasn't sure what to expect at all. I felt like the guppy in a pond similar to the Central Park Reservoir. However, I refused to let my disoriented past translate into a disoriented future. Surely, the other interns in the program would have prior internship experience under their belts. Clearly, I didn't. But I wasn't about to advertise that to the whole world. I needed to start on a powerful note. I needed to be memorable in the best way possible.

"Ma'am?" a man's voice asked from outside my thought bubble. I readjusted my stance and vision to see who was talking to me. "Ma'am, you've been standing in front of this building for over 15 minutes now. Are you all right?"

"Oh! No, I'm fine," I responded in a flustered tone. "I start a new internship at Jarvis Advertising and Marketing in a few days. I was just trying to figure out my route ahead of time. It's in this building on the eighth floor."

"I know it's on the eighth floor," the man said. "I'm one of the doormen for this building. My name is Henry."

"I'm Josefina. It's nice to meet you, Henry."

Henry was an older man with silver streaks throughout his neatly combed hair. He wore a suit like any other man, only he wore a brass, engraved name tag that read: Henry Horne, Building Doorman. Wrinkles on his face seemed to symbolize all the stories he could tell from working in this building. He had both laugh lines and frown lines, which made me believe that his life was filled with heartbreak and joy, with joy winning out in the end. He took my hand and led me under the building's large awning.

"It's going to rain soon," he said. "Don't want you getting soggy now."

Already, Henry was looking out for me and I hadn't even started the internship yet.

"Thank you, Henry," I said. "It will be nice to be able to start on Monday and see a familiar face when I walk in these doors."

Just then, it began to downpour. What was it about me and this place that summoned the rain gods?

"How did you know it was going to rain right now?" I asked like a skeptic of voodoo magic.

He chuckled an old man's chuckle. "My knees are the best weathervane you'll ever find. I have a feeling this one is going to last a while. If you don't want to wait it out, I'll get you an umbrella."

I peered into the wall of rain that was created before me by the awning. It reminded me of the summer storm I encountered when I first interviewed at J.A.M. It was one of those storms that wasn't going to let up too soon.

"I think I'll wait it out for a little while here, if that's all right?"

"That's more than all right. I like the company," Henry approved. "Manning this front desk and lobby can be lonesome."

"I can understand that."

I took a seat on a stool beside the front desk. Henry shared some of the stories that I believed aged and renewed him. He told me about his time fighting in the Korean War and how he moved to New York City from Houston, Texas following his military service. "That's where I needed to be," he said. In his eyes, at the time, New York was the land of opportunity. He said that he started out working in a bubble gum factory doing brunt work for little pay. After over 10 years of working in the factory, when he saved up enough money, he started his own business – a hardware store near Washington Square. Eventually, big box hardware stores infiltrated the market so when Henry's hardware store closed in 1990, he heard from a friend that there was a doorman position available in this building, so he took it.

"I loved my hardware store. It was a great place to meet new people in the neighborhood. But times change and you have to move on," Henry reminisced.

"You can meet people in the building too, right?" I inquired.

"Sure. Sure, although most people are in a hurry or on the phone. I see new people every day, but very few take the time. It can get lonely." He paused for a moment. "If you hadn't been standing outside for almost 20 minutes staring up at the sky like a loon, I wouldn't have met you. Eventually, you would have rushed off somewhere else, and you would just be part of a sea of faces walking through those doors come Monday."

I thought about that for a whole minute. Henry was right. I needed to make time to get to know people in New York; this city was going to seem awfully lonely, awfully fast. That would be my first New York Resolution: Meet new people on a regular basis.

"You are so right, Henry."

Henry and I shared stories for a few hours, until I noticed it was getting dark. The rain had stopped and all that was left were reflections of light in puddles on the pavement, which were perfect for jumping in. I told Henry that I had to go; I still needed to buy some groceries or else have nothing to eat. I knew I would see him again on Monday for my first day at Jarvis Advertising and Marketing. Bonding with Henry made me feel comforted about the new transition to being a working person, but anxiety was still looming over my thoughts. Luckily, the puddles outside invited me to hop through on my way back to the subway. I had to remember to take a downtown train. I didn't want to end up somewhere like Harlem, which seemed to constantly be featured on news broadcasts for less than positive things. However, I had never actually been to Harlem or anywhere above 70th Street. I wasn't actually sure how to get to Harlem at that point either. All I knew was I lived at 16 Clinton Street, off Delancey Street, downtown, near the Williamsburg Bridge, which led to another unknown place. The unknown was in my midst. It surrounded me and engulfed me. There was so much left to learn. I wasn't in Jersey anymore.

CHAPTER TWELVE

"Beware the barrenness of a busy life." – Socrates

Waking up at 7:30 a.m. to be at Jarvis Advertising and Marketing was a challenge after going through most of the summer season waking up closer to noon everyday. My alarm clock sounded like death. After taking a shower in my neon green tiled bathroom, I realized that I still hadn't quite adjusted to living with someone else. By the time I finished drying my hair and opened the bathroom door, Regina was standing there with her towel in tow waiting for her turn to use the facilities. Apparently, I spent too long in there. Oops.

There was something about first days that is embedded in our being since elementary school. It was imperative to have the coolest first day outfit. If you looked like a loser on the first day, it was assumed that you would be labeled as a loser for the rest of elementary school, if not through middle school. This was the tradition I was used to. I only hoped that if I looked my best on my first day at J.A.M., I would have a better chance of being accepted. However, I wasn't so used to New Yorker style, so my best New Jersey style would have to do. I decided on a dark blue skirt and a white button-down shirt. Shoes were more of an issue mostly because for some reason, I couldn't find half of them. I kept searching for these black heels my mother gave me. They went perfectly with the outfit I had chosen, but for some reason, they weren't in the box I thought I had packed them in. Hence, I hopped from box to box, frantically searching out these patent leather pumps that I desperately needed to wear to my first day or else be ostracized for the rest of this six-month internship. Eventually, I found them, noticed I was running late, plucked a banana off the kitchen counter, and paused for a moment to make sure I had everything I needed for the day. When that was confirmed, I grabbed my keys and headed out into the great yonder of the working world.

I made my way to the subway station only to be met with a rather large crowd waiting for the train on the platform. I had a feeling my bubble of personal space was about to be invaded by the downtown commuters heading to work uptown. And I was right. As soon as the F train arrived, people immediately attacked the opening doorways. Full of nervousness about this situation, I followed suit and joined the commuter chaos. The conductor of the train had to make an announcement for boarding passengers to allow leaving passengers to actually leave the train before boarding themselves. I was going to need to get used to this morning excitement. In my mind, it was far too early to deal with situations like this. There was no available seat on the train, which meant that I would have to balance myself standing in high heels on a moving train – a sight to behold! I wasn't used to wearing heels in the first place. Getting to the subway station without falling over was a challenge of its own. Finding a way to maintain a standing position while not completely embarrassing myself was going to be an interesting experience, despite my tight grip on one of the stability poles inside the train. Luckily, after witnessing me struggle all the way to the 2nd Avenue stop, a nice stranger got up and offered me his seat. I thanked him and he simply held onto one of the poles and rode along without any sign of a struggle to stand during the bumpy train ride. I thought, *If he can manage to do that with such ease, I'll get there too.* Somehow, I felt that there was hope for me in New York City.

When the subway train stopped at 23rd Street, I walked with that New York City stride (or at least my imitation of it) toward the street exit. I adopted a determined pace toward the J.A.M. office building. Bethany texted me an encouraging message as I arrived at my destination:

BETHANY: Good Luck Today Bestie!! :)

I needed all the luck I could get. Upon opening the large, glass front doors, Henry gave me a warm, welcoming greeting, which set the tone for the rest of my day. Then, he directed me toward the elevator bank where I met a couple other new interns also headed to the eighth floor. One was named Brian, a rather tall person with tightly wound curly brown hair, looking like a confident professional wearing a dark grey suit and a red tie. Georgina was the less flashy, more down to earth-looking intern wearing a purple dress and black flats. The elevator went *ding* so we got on to ascend to the J.A.M. offices as potential competitors and potential friends.

"You look sharp," I commented to Brian.

"This *is* an ad agency. You need to look the part," he responded with an overconfident, snarky tone while simultaneously judging me.

That's when everyone decided to share which school they attended. The listing went as follows:

Georgina: New York University
Brian: Rutgers University
Me: Princeton University

It turned out Brian and I grew up in towns very near to each other. One would think we would make a friendly connection after that. One would be wrong. Brian had his game face on and in his mind, he was going to win this non-existent reality competition show that we had all signed up for. He was on another level, convinced that we weren't worthy or capable of doing work comparable to his. The energy in the elevator got super tense so when the elevator went *ding* again, I was sure we were all desperate and eager to escape that elevator cab and move forward to our first day experiences.

First, we were ushered into a conference room for an introductory meeting with directors of each department in the agency. Xavier Underwood was head of Marketing, Joan Smiley was in charge of the

Advertising department, and Donna Majesco was the leader of the Public Relations team.

Joan Smiley (who I had spoken with on the phone once), started out the meeting by saying, "This will be a unique and challenging experience for all of you. Each of you will spend two months working under Xavier, Donna, or myself in our respective departments in a rotation style. Not all of you will excel in each discipline, and that is okay. The point of this process is for you to learn where your individual strengths and talents fit best. Our job is to lead you, as interns, toward your future careers in the world of advertising, marketing, and public relations."

It sounded like some speech she had rehearsed time and time again. She had the dynamics and fluidity of it down to a science. My old public speaking professor would have loved to have her as an example of how it's done.

Then, it was Xavier Underwood's turn to speak, "Donna here is handing out your rotation schedules for the next six months."

"You will be in rotation teams," Donna Majesco interjected as she passed around our assignments. "These teams will be your groups for monthly projects and presentations."

"So get ready for an internship like you've never had before," Xavier Underwood adjourned the meeting on a strong note.

All of the interns looked around the large conference table to size up the others. There was a moment of silence for that until Xavier Underwood interrupted the awkwardness and told us to move on to our respective departments. My rotation schedule read that I would start with marketing with Xavier Underwood. He was a slightly intimidating man, tall with a well-groomed goatee. Rather than get lost in this office that looked like a labyrinth, I followed him out of the conference room to a smaller workroom that would fit the three interns in my rotation team. Georgina caught up with me to see which team I was in. Apparently, she was in the same group as me.

"I really hope that Brian guy isn't in our group," she said. "He wasn't the most endearing person. First impressions make a difference to me. I have a hard time working with people who simply can't be nice to other people – especially people they just met."

"Totally," I replied. "This shouldn't be such a cutthroat program. It's not like they're cutting people. Right?"

"Right. But these projects they assign are going to be tough. I know it."

This girl seemed like a sharpshooter. She had already sized everyone up and figured she would befriend me. It was a nice way to start my first day. Georgina and I sat next to each other at the round table. She told me about the advertising classes she took at NYU and how she was a member of some student marketing organizations on campus. I decided not to disclose my extreme lack of experience in this field at the moment and instead, I told her about my recent move to the city.

"I've lived here my whole life in different neighborhoods over the years," Georgina gushed. "But I've never lived on the Lower East Side. I always party down there. It's such a cool spot."

"Thanks," I responded. "It's good to know straight from a New Yorker that I didn't move to the armpit of the city."

She laughed. "Isn't Jersey the armpit of the country, though?"

"Oh, yeah. People call it that, but it's not really –"

"I think you're past those armpit days."

I had to believe her. My "armpit days" were far behind me. I moved to New York City on my own, was living with my first roommate, did my own grocery shopping (sometimes), was paying my own rent, and had my first sort-of job. I may have been known as a forever-kid back home, but I was in an adult world and I refused to fail. I suddenly understood why Brian was being such a d-bag. He was from New Jersey too and he had a lot to prove in this internship, as did I.

"Okay, everyone," Xavier Underwood entered the glass room and addressed his first rotation of interns. "I don't believe in summer camp style introductions. I'll learn your names and who you all are based on your work and your interactions with me and your peers here. If I don't know who you are by the end of this two-month rotation, shame on you. There are only three of you here. So take initiative. Understood?"

The trio of interns who sat around the table complied with enthusiasm. We were informed that we were on first name basis with our mentor. Xavier also assigned our first group project. He wanted us to do some market research on a new product for a client J.A.M. had just signed on with. We were instructed to develop a series of questions and ask passersby to answer our survey.

"Your market research classes in college should have covered this method, so I expect nothing less than exceptional work," Xavier said. He was a tough love pep talker.

Clearly, I had never taken a market research class in my life, nor did I know how to create a survey for this type of purpose. I was a philosophy major – not a psychology major. Theories were my thing so if my team needed a consult on analyzing whatever data we collected, I was totally down for turning my Aristotle thinking helmet on. However, the mere thought of attempting to fool these people who actually studied marketing in college that I had a clue about this process was terrifying. I wasn't a good actor – I tried in a class play in elementary school once. Never again. I played a piece of celery; ironically, kids in the audience – my fellow classmates – boo-ed me during my singing solo to the point that they started throwing little bags of baby carrots at me. Regardless of my past critics' actions, I decided to take the leap into my new role as a fraudulent intern.

"Okay, team. Let's brainstorm," Leon, a blonde, trendy guy with large black-rimmed glasses in my group, jump started the discussion.

Our assigned product was a new face cleanser from a well-known cosmetics company that I had never heard of. Apparently, I was the only one not in the know. I got some weird looks from the rest of my team. Despite my lack of familiarity with the brand, I was determined to find a way to contribute to the pow wow, or organizational meeting. I didn't know where to start, so I let Leon and Georgina begin. My plan was to interject helpful comments of wisdom as a way to contribute. These helpful comments of wisdom were intended to be shared only after I had a better idea of what market research was and how exactly we were supposed to collect it.

"Well, I think we should set up our research objectives first," Leon contributed, sounding like he knew what he was talking about. I couldn't tell the difference.

"Objectives are good. Let's make a list," Georgina took charge. "Josefina, can you take notes on whatever ideas for the objectives we come up with?"

I gulped, but knew this meant all I had to do was write things down. My eyes must have looked like they were bugging out of my head, but I calmed it down and managed to say, "Sure."

My teammates began throwing out suggestions for the main objectives of the research as I jotted down everything almost verbatim. I got really good at that during Professor Dawson's Latin Works of Literature class my sophomore year. He had a way of talking in a stream of consciousness type of way, always finding a way to sneak in some important analysis that I needed to know for the final exam. It meant that I needed to transcribe his lectures as he spoke and sometimes mumbled. I learned how to decipher his mumbling with an accent as well as recite Latin poetry and prose like a pro. However, in this case, Latin literature probably wasn't the most useful knowledge to have. I knew nothing about this subject matter and I feared my peers would figure it out sooner than later. I hoped I could get through this first project without blowing my cover.

"We need to identify the target market," Leon ordered.

"Target market" seemed like something I read about marketing on the Internet. It was one of those marketing buzzwords. I also realized I had not spoken a word toward the productivity of this conversation.

"Yes! I think the target market is a really important, um, aspect of this project," I called out as a way of reminding my team that I was still in the conference room and hadn't completely checked out into dreamland. I was getting there, though.

"Okay," Leon said in a calm and calculated tone. "Our product is a face cleanser."

"So then, um, who is our target market?" I asked.

Leon said, "Isn't it obvious? It's women."

"Don't be such a guy, Leon," Georgina quipped. "Face cleansers are for men, too, you know."

I mustered up some courage and decided to be brave. I spoke up. "She's right. My cousin Felix had really bad acne when he was a teenager so he started using a face cleanser, I forget which one it was, he told me once, but he's a dude and he uses a face cleanser. Maybe we should consider including men in this research."

Leon considered my reasoning for a few moments and finally gave in to including men respondents in the project. I was proud. Maybe it wasn't so far fetched that I was interning at major marketing firm not ever having any formal education about the field. Something about me was promising enough for the directors of Jarvis Advertising and Marketing to decide to give me a try in this program. Only time would tell, but this was a good start.

My first day at J.A.M. turned out to be a success. Or at least I felt it was. Everyone in the internship was on some level of high-strung. The first week was going by rather quickly, but the days felt long and arduous. I was learning at least 117 new things every day. It was like marketing boot camp. By the time I got back to my apartment, I would just drag myself to my bedroom and collapse on my bed. Regina would say, "Good morning, sleeping beauty," as a sarcastic joke because I always seemed to be so tired. Aside from some texting conversations, I hadn't actually seen Malcolm all week. I felt guilty leaving him out to dry like that. Bethany found I was being distant. She kept calling me to see how my first week was and I was so preoccupied that I would forget to call her back. My mom and dad called a few times during the week to make sure I was still alive, to which I always answered, "I'm still breathing and I still have a heartbeat." That was my stock answer to that inquiry. I should have made that my voice mail message: "You've reached Josefina Ruiz's phone. I'm not available at the moment, but I am still breathing with a heartbeat. Leave a message after the tone and I'll get back to you when I'm not working or catching up on sleep." That would have been clever. I did feel bad that I was unintentionally alienating the most important people in my life. I feared I would end up alone in my apartment. Regina would be the only person who had any contact with me solely because otherwise she would have to find another place to live that would cost her twice the rent she was paying with me. I was starting to really understand true loneliness. Where was a swing set when I needed one?

Once my team's research proposal and survey were completed and approved by Xavier, we went to Times Square to have people who fit our target market answer the survey. Imagine the overwhelming crowds in Times Square. Millions of people travel through or entertain themselves in this city center. That said, we took a no-teammate-left-behind approach. We figured that a group that sticks together, wins together. That's what we figured. After being completely ignored by passersby, almost getting trampled by a herd of teenage girls who thought they had a celebrity sighting of their favorite movie star (to be honest, I thought I saw the same celebrity), and relocating after being told by a police officer that we weren't allowed to stand in the middle of Times Square soliciting surveys at tourists, our final tally of completed surveys by relevant respondents was: three. And two of them could be considered questionable.

Georgina had the attitude that we just needed to come back the next week and try again with a new strategy. That's all we could do. That, and go out on the town Saturday night. I hadn't had the chance to check out the New York City nightlife. Honestly, I was terrified of being out at night in the city and going out to a bar alone was just pathetic and sad. Georgina said she knew a guy who was a promoter at some club in the Meatpacking District (as if I knew where that was) and that he could get us in to have some Saturday night fun. I agreed to go on the condition that Malcolm could accompany me.

Looking through my closet to find an outfit for Saturday night, I noticed I was not prepared with any nightlife outfits – especially not any appropriate for New York City nightlife. Out of desperate need for something to wear, I resorted to asking a favor from my roommate. I always hated asking for help with seemingly simple tasks. So I took a deep breath and a loud sigh and dragged my feet next door to Regina's room. She was on the phone with Roy and rather than disturb her conversation with her boyfriend, I turned around and back to my room.

"Josefina?" she called out to me.

Surprised that she interrupted whatever nonsense Roy had to say, I turned right back around.

"Did you need something? You should really go food shopping when you're hungry and have, like, nothing in the fridge, you know? No one else is going to do it for you and I'm not giving you any more of my yogurts."

I sighed. "I'm not hungry. I don't need your food."

"Okay," Regina said furrowing her eyebrows out of confusion. She held her hand over the microphone to her phone to exclude Roy from the awkward roommate discussion.

I already hated asking her for help with anything, but usually, I would ask her if I could have one of her precious yogurts if I was fresh out of food and was too lazy or tired to go shopping. I felt like asking for something else was only going to add to that mental list of all the yogurts I owed her.

"This girl in my group at the internship, Georgina, she has an in at a club in the Meatpacking District and she's invited me and a few other people to go out with her tonight, the thing is I don't have anything to wear that looks appropriate for clubbing or whatever in New York, but I know you have lots of things for going out and so I was wondering if I could borrow something of yours for the night because I think you have such a good sense of style," I said avoiding eye contact and cringing at my use of a ridiculous run-on sentence. It was as if I didn't come up for air until I complimented her 'sense of style' through my teeth.

Regina took that compliment to heart and sported the widest grin on her face. She unsilenced her phone and said, "Roy, I'm gonna have to call you back." Then, she jumped off her bed in one swift motion, went to the open doorway I was standing in, grabbed my hands to pull me into her room, and said, "I have waiting to do a makeover on you since I met you! This is going to be so much fun!"

I became her little project. She had me try on all sorts of different outfits, mostly sparkly, sequins, and metallics always paired with something black. It was impossible to not notice all the glitter that shed off her clothes and onto every surface. Then, there were the one-shoulder tops, tank tops, tube tops, and halter-tops. I got a crash course in clubbing fashion.

By the time Malcolm showed up at my door, Regina had done my makeup, "fixed" my hair (as she put it), and dressed me up to the nines. I also had nine-inch heels on – or at least it felt that way. Standing, let alone walking, dancing, or any other type of movement was going to be a challenge.

"Hi, Malcolm. Josefina will be out in a sec. You won't believe your eyes! I gave her a makeover! Just wait," Regina said as she hustled Malcolm into our still barren living room. It literally had no furniture. It was just a living room with no living in it.

I was horrified at how I looked. If my mother saw someone looking the way I did, she would say, "*¡Qué puta!*" If the tramp look was coming back in style, I should have been on the cover of the magazine – every magazine. Eventually, after examining my going out ensemble, I emerged from my room to face Malcolm. I expected him to laugh. I really did. I expected him to be rolling over in hysterics. Instead, when I made eye contact with him, he nodded. No words. Just a nod.

"Good work, Regina," he said.

"Are you serious?" I said being completely shocked by his seemingly serious reaction to this travesty of a makeover. I was wearing so much glitter that I reflected light like a Disco ball.

Regina, full of pride in her work as though I was some painting or sculpture she had been slaving over all day, said, "She looks good, right?"

"She looks great."

Malcolm could not keep his eyes off me. Maybe it was all the sparkle. I was still confused by his belief that how I looked was appropriate for anything, let alone some ritzy club in the Meatpacking District.

"Seriously?" I asked again just to make sure he hadn't gone temporarily insane.

"Go have fun, you two! Just remember, don't do anything I wouldn't do," Regina imparted her encouraging words for us with a giggle.

When we reached the front stoop for my building, we both started looking both ways down the street, though it was a one-way street.

"So how do we get to the Meatpacking District?" I admitted my ignorance.

"Well, we can start by taking a cab," Malcolm responded.

"A cab?"

"Yep. A cab. We have to go to Delancey if we want to catch one," Malcolm instructed and took a few steps in that direction and then stopped. "Can you walk in those?"

He noticed I was still standing in place. Walking down the stairs was a death trap in itself, but at least there was something drilled into the wall to hold on to. Malcolm was on my other arm, so I had double safety harnesses. On the street, it was going to be a little tougher. I was bound to break my ankle, both ankles, or my neck attempting to make baby steps in the direction of anywhere. I just stood there, trying to be cute and batting my fake eyelashes at him.

"Okay," he said as he walked back to me. Then, he linked arms with me and stepped slowly with me toward Delancey Street to catch a cab. I nearly wiped out on the sidewalk a few times. I'm pretty sure some people laughed at me.

Riding in a New York City taxi cab was a new adventure for me. Malcolm stepped into the street with his arm outstretched in order to hail a cab while I stayed back trying to balance myself in Regina's stilt-heels. After a few minutes, Malcolm was able to flag one down and he helped me get into the cab without falling awkwardly into the back seat. We told the cab driver where we were headed and off we went. I saw the city from streets I hadn't wandered yet. Seeing Manhattan in the dark didn't seem so scary after all. It seemed as though the whole city was out on the streets. It was a beautiful night – not too cool and not too hot and muggy for the end of the summer – perfect. Neon lights from bars, car headlights, and street lamps twinkled and illuminated the streets. As we arrived into the trendy Meatpacking District, I was suddenly thankful that Regina had dressed me up as she did. As overkill as it seemed at the time, my made over look seemed to be just right for this nightlife crowd. Somehow I looked less trampy when I was suddenly surrounded by other girls who were also clearly going all out and dressed to impress. I was so used to campus parties where you were expected to step it up a bit, but I always had Bethany to borrow from for an appropriate outfit. It was a little harder to do that now living across the Hudson River in different states.

Stepping outside of the cab was a challenge when I didn't notice that the ground beneath me was cobblestone rather than paved. I held on to the taxi cab for support until Malcolm could help me regain some semblance of balance.

"Josefina! You made it!" I heard Georgina squeal from a distance. I couldn't quite figure out where her voice was coming from. There were a number of different clubs and bars on the block, each with their own lengthy lines that wrapped around corners and then some. I was looking for the Masquerade Club. "Josefina! Over here!"

I tried to follow the sound and eventually, after almost completely wiping out several times as a result of the deadly combination of stilt-heels and cobblestone streets, I found Georgina. In order to reach her, I grabbed Malcolm's arm to help me get to her without breaking both of my ankles.

"Josefina! I'm so glad you made it out," Georgina greeted me. "And who is this man on your arm?" She greeted Malcolm.

"Actually, I think she's on *my* arm," Malcolm joked as he introduced himself to my new internship-work friend.

Georgina ushered us in line beside her. The line went around the block and I was skeptical that we would make it inside the club before midnight, which was already way past my bedtime. Georgina was waiting for some of her other friends to arrive and join us, but in the meantime, she was intent on making my virgin New York City club night a "brilliant success," as she stated several times. I really didn't want to mention to Georgina that I never properly celebrated my 21st birthday, but when she asked me what I did to commemorate the milestone, I revealed that I sat in the kitchen of my parents' house sifting through employment opportunities with hopes that I would find something I actually might enjoy working in.

"Oh. My. GOD!" Georgina squealed and startled everybody in line with us within a 10-person radius. "This is going to be so much fun!" she said giddily as she began hopping up and down in her sky-high gold sandals. "Josefina, I can't believe you never celebrated your 21st! It's a rite of passage. It's not like turning 22 or 23. Those years basically mean nothing. This is a big deal!"

"It's really not a big deal," I said, sneaking a look at Malcolm.

"Do you think this is a big deal, Malcolm? I mean, your girlfriend here never celebrated her 21st birthday out and about," she continued. "This is a travesty! Tonight, we will right this wrong and make this city our playground!" Georgina roared, catching the attention of everyone within a five-foot radius of our position in line. "I really need a drink though. This line better start moving soon."

Eventually, we made it to the front of the line at around 12:15 a.m., which was still past my bedtime. Regardless, my new friend Georgina had clear intentions to make my belated birthday dreams come true. Georgina knew the club promoter and we were able to get in without paying the 50 dollar cover. The bouncer looked at me funny as I awkwardly fumbled with my ID, even though I was a bona fide, legal adult.

The Masquerade Club was worthy of its name. It looked like one of those grand masquerade balls that we see in movies. There were extravagant curtains highlighted by dim mood lighting, a black and white checkered dance floor filled with people moving to the beat of the DJ's playlist. Black leather couches created a separation from the dancing space to the mingling area. It was nothing like the college parties I was used to. The floor wasn't sticky and there wasn't a red plastic cup in sight.

"Come on!" Georgina grabbed my wrist and led me through the crowd to the bar. Poor Malcolm was just dragging behind me making sure my face didn't hit the floor. I had a few close calls on the stilts Regina loaned me. Upon arriving at the bar, Georgina took one look at the bartender and immediately made flirty goo goo eyes at him.

"It's my friend's birthday," she called across the bar loud enough so he could hear her over the loud music. "She needs a drink!"

And just like that, the bartender whose name I came to learn was Bobby had three colorful drinks laid out on the bar. Georgina passed one to me to hand off to Malcolm.

"What is this?" Malcolm asked after a quick sip of his pink and blue drink. He inspected the glass and took a few more sips attempting to make an educated guess as to the cocktail's ingredients. "I definitely think the blue part is curacao, but the pink part … I just don't know. It's damn tasty though."

"Hey, Bobby!" Georgina summoned our bartender who had moved on to the opposite side of the space to tend to some scantily clad women who looked like they were getting a little too old to be wearing such skimpy outfits. Bobby smoothly walked over to our corner of the bar.

"What's up? Don't like your drinks?" our sleeve-tattooed mixologist addressed us as he was simultaneously serving up drinks for the women attempting to hold onto their youth.

"No, they're very … fruity. What's in them?"

"Ah. There's some grenadine, gin, club soda, some strawberries and blackberries, and some blue curacao for color and kick," Bobby explained. He glanced at me over Georgina's shoulder, looked me up and down, and said, "Happy Birthday. It's on the house. Go have fun."

Despite being in a crowded club with loud club music that kept repeating the phrase "drop the bass", and the fact that I was wearing an outfit I found completely ridiculous and impractical for dancing – considering Malcolm was basically my crutch to stay upright – and being in this environment with my boyfriend (still unbelievable) and a new friend, something still felt like it was missing. It finally occurred to me that this new experience in a New York City dance club was missing my favorite dance partner: Bethany.

"Hold this," I gave Malcolm my fruity-gin-and-tonic-con-curacao birthday drink.

In a glance, I noticed that he was almost done drinking the pink concoction in his glass, but I ignored it for a moment and proceeded to take my phone out of the green sequined bag Regina loaned me for the night. "Ugh! Why isn't there any freaking reception in here?"

"Who are you trying to call?" Malcolm asked.

"Come on, Josefina! Forget that. You can call whomever you want later. Now is dancing time!" Georgina chimed in rather loudly, grabbed my wrist and pulled me onto the dance floor with her. Malcolm wasn't far behind, still holding my drink and slurping up his own.

Soon, I was overtaken by the thumping beat of the DJ's playlist. I started to get lost in the sound and the energy from the dance floor permeated my concern that I hadn't talked to Bethany in two weeks, which was a long time for us. Then, Rihanna's "Umbrella" played on the speaker system. Memories from my days at Princeton, going to parties and Bethany getting completely sloshed on a problematic intoxicating concoction and singing this silly song like the quintessential drunk girl at college parties began flooding back. It was also an image I had seen so many times in movies about characters living up their college years with no regrets or shame. That's what I used to prepare for my first day at college. Starting a year younger than most undergraduate freshman, I always felt I needed to supplement my experience, especially since I commuted from home everyday. It just wasn't the same. When I met Bethany at orientation, I knew I found a friend for life. I was near the level of distraught just remembering that I had been so busy with my internship and my new life that I had almost forgotten to reach out to my best friend. Eventually, my inner thoughts had superseded my excitement over finally celebrating my 21st birthday with Georgina and Malcolm. They both noticed that I was distracted by something when I almost bit the dust in those freaking shoes I just *had* to borrow.

"Whoa. Whoa," Malcolm grabbed me just in time so I didn't have to live through the embarrassment of falling over while simply standing and attempting to keep my unstable feet in place while I swayed to the music. Luckily, he had already put the glasses of our rainbow drinks down (after he finished his, he finished mine for me) so he was free to catch me like the Prince Charming he was.

As Malcolm steadied me, Georgina found us a small, black, loungey leather couch to sit on.

"Ok. I know you didn't have that much of that crazy drink," Georgina kneeled in front of me to take the evil shoes off my feet. "Are you all right?"

135

"What happened out there? You were up and then you were falling," Malcolm stroked my hair with concern.

"I don't know. I guess I just lost my balance with Regina's shoes," I lied. "I'm fine really. These shoes literally want to kill me, though."

"Well, every 21st birthday party should involve the birthday girl almost or completely wiping out somewhere," Georgina stayed optimistic about my minor celebration *faux pas*. "I'd say this was a success. What do you say we call it a night? We do have a crazy week ahead of us at J.A.M. These presentations are going to be the death of me. We should get some rest. What do you say?"

Interning at J.A.M. was taking a toll on me as well. There was a lot of pressure. I was so focused on being dedicated to the projects and assignments that were expected of me that I was beginning to forget about everyone important in my life. My mother called me every day and every day I was just too busy to take even ten minutes and update her on my day. My inbox was so flooded with e-mails from my dad. I had skimmed through some of them mentioning that he and my mom were going to Puerto Rico for a vacation or something soon. Still, I simply didn't have the time or energy to answer with a substantial response. And I had lost touch with Bethany over the past few weeks. I felt terrible about that. I felt guilty about leaving her out to dry like that, but I was just suddenly so preoccupied with career-type things in my new New York life that I was beginning to lose sight of who I was before when I was sitting on my parents' couch watching romantic comedies and dramas that would entertain me while I did nothing with my life. This was a change I needed to start adjusting to in a healthy way. If I was going to have this new life with actual career aspirations, I was going to need to preserve who I was before. Losing sight of who the original Josefina Ruiz was would not be a desired after effect of an internship, a job, or a city.

I looked at Malcolm and asked him if he would take me home. I honestly couldn't even fathom how I would get back to the Lower East Side. A savvy New Yorker, I was not. Yet.

CHAPTER THIRTEEN

"All paid jobs absorb and degrade the mind." – Aristotle

It was time for our next cycle. My team was assigned to the Public Relations department with Donna Majesco. Xavier's cycle was like a crash course in marketing, especially since all I knew about it was from books I had glanced at while camping out in the Bellcastle Public Library. I still felt completely underprepared for any of the aspects of this internship. Despite the fact that I knew I was definitely learning from the experience even after a few weeks, I was still unsure that this was the career for me. So while I was working on a new skill set and knowledge base, I was doubtful that I would ever become a successful marketer. Georgina seemed better suited for this career. She was a real go-getter. She had a way of making people listen. I was organized and cerebral, which got me stuck most of the time. I was creative with a top-notch imagination, but I hadn't found the best place to apply those qualities at J.A.M. yet.

I took my seat at the conference table in between Georgina and Leon at 9:00 AM. By 10:30 AM, all three of us had reached capacity on the principles of Public Relations, which Donna Majesco still wasn't done explaining. She had a PowerPoint presentation prepared to show us how to develop a PR plan, how to write a press release, how to effectively and professionally communicate with clients and publics (as she called them), and a number of other things that appeared in slides 47 through 72. By the end, it was all a blur, and the three of us really could have used a coffee break. It was possibly the most exhausting lecture I had ever endured -- and I survived eight semesters of Philosophy, Classic Literature, and History courses at an Ivy League university. Somehow, I was starting to feel like that thirst for knowledge was slowly dying. My brain was so occupied with doing work and getting tangible results that I was starting to lose sight of what I was really looking for when I started my initial job search back in June. At the beginning of October, I could barely keep my eyes open long enough to catch a glimpse of a slide that Donna had projected. Maybe I simply wasn't interested in working in Public Relations. Maybe I was just tired. I didn't know. What I did know was that Jarvis Advertising and Marketing was paying me to do work and that was what I was going to do.

"All right," Donna said as she flipped on the lights. "Any questions about this first assignment?"

I immediately panicked. I was too busy philosophizing about my life and what had become of it to actually listen to Donna's introduction of our project. I was terrified of asking her to repeat herself. That would be embarrassing. I could feel myself sweating. Georgina and Leon would likely fill in the missing pieces from my limited memory of the explanation, but I anticipated Donna leaning over the conference table to be in my face over catching me daydream during her presentation. I may have been losing my mind, but I still knew how to play along. All of my 21 years of prioritizing youth over maturity taught me some very valuable lessons. Lesson One: Even if you go into Dream Land, always appear to be paying attention. The way I perfected this technique had gotten me out of so many issues with professors at Princeton. Being sweet and cute helps, too. That's classic.

Luckily, Donna didn't seem to notice that my mind was elsewhere. If she did, she certainly didn't mention it. I didn't need to use my forever-kid skills that morning.

"All right," Donna continued. "Get to work."

Then, she departed for her own desk to get real work done. I was left with Georgina and Leon.

"So, who is our client again?" I asked hesitantly.

"Were you even paying attention to the PowerPoint?" Leon squawked at me.

I looked at him like a deer in headlights for a moment, unable to quickly think of how to recover. I was beginning to notice a lapse in my forever-kid skills. *Think fast, Josefina. ¡Rapido!*

"Are you accusing me of not paying attention?" I snapped. "I'm shocked, Leon. I have been here one hundred and ten percent all morning. I'm just asking a simple question about our client. Is that all right with you?"

Leon looked at me with squinted eyes and then he apologized for his tone. Georgina provided me with the answer to my initial question.

"The client here is this fashion company. They're called Blossom & Bloom. From what I gather, they design dresses. Apparently, they have a new collection coming out."

Great, I thought sarcastically. Fashion was one thing I felt really behind the eight-ball with. I was so used to ultra-casual wear like T-shirts, sweatshirts, jeans, and sneakers. I had acquired a few pair of flats that were fancier and exactly two pair of high heels. Both were black. I rarely wore dresses. I had very few of them. My style was simplistic, exuding a blatant lack of interest in style to the world. In New York City, that was like a crime against humanity.

"Okay. So fashion," I said. "I'm not the expert on that, but I'm sure we could come up with a few ideas for Blossom & Bloom."

Leon was first to suggest points of action for us to propose to Donna. Georgina, always the enthusiastic work horse, joined in with strategy and logistics. I sat there at the conference table attempting to look like I was taking notes in another world, only observing my teammates think up a storm. None of this sparked any light in me that would motivate me to strive to work in this career and live in this lifestyle. I was pretty sure that quickly losing interest in things was a textbook quality of those in my condition as a forever-kid. I still wasn't ready to grow up. A regular paycheck didn't even make me feel more like an adult.

Then, my phone rang in my bag. I thought I had set it on silent, though technically, it was supposed to be off. It couldn't be one of those light buzzes or quiet ringtones. Of course, my phone had to make that loud buzz, obnoxious ring that reverberated so everyone on the floor could hear. I immediately reached for it and tried to turn off the volume so it wouldn't disturb the entire floor nine times over. Leon and Georgina shot looks at me that made my cheeks feel like they were on fire. When I finally got the sound to turn off, Donna rushed into the glassed in conference room in the middle of the eighth floor. Trouble.

"I heard a very loud noise come from this conference room," Donna began her scolding. "Whose was it? Which one of you?"

Brian and Georgina turned their heads in my direction. My cheeks were rising in temperature.

"Josefina, you know the policy about phones here. You can have it, but I don't want to see it and I certainly don't want to hear it – especially when it sounds like that monstrosity. This is not high school, so I will not take it away from you. That's silly and unnecessary. So *please* do not let that happen again. Understood?"

I nodded politely. My face felt like *fuego* at this point.

"All right then. What ideas have you three come up with so far?"

She listened to the ideas that Leon and Georgina came up with. They had elaborate plans for this public relations campaign for Bloom & Blossom. I felt completely out of the conversation so I reverted to the classic smile and nod technique for appearing enthusiastic while really not having the slightest interest in the topic being discussed. My mind was elsewhere.

Eventually, after drilling us with questions about my team's proposed plan for our client, Donna retreated back to her office, but not without giving me a quick look before leaving the conference room. I sighed out of relief that I wasn't thrown out of the internship program simply because my phone essentially detonated this awful sound that blew up in the office. No one was spared, but somehow I was the only survivor.

On my way out the office, Georgina told me to get my act together. Leon piggybacked on that comment and said, "Yeah, we need one hundred and fifty percent of you tomorrow."

I responded with an, "Uh huh. Got it," and hopped on the elevator. I greeted Henry at the front desk hoping he had a smoother day than I. It occurred to me that I didn't check to see who called me in that unfortunate moment of wrong place, wrong time, wrong phone. It was my dad. He would never call me during my workday. He knew how strict they were about personal phone calls. He left a voicemail, but the city streets were so noisy with trucks and honking cars and obnoxiously loud people that I couldn't make out most of what he was saying. I would have to wait until I got home to the Lower East Side to call him back.

———

The subway ride home was rather loud – louder than usual. Aside from the regular screeching of the train grinding against the steel tracks, to my right was a mother trying to get her two young kids to stop screaming at each other over the I'm-not-touching-you game. On my left, was a group of men less than harmoniously harmonizing to "Amazing Grace," which they repeated the entire time I was on the train as if we asked for an encore. There was a couple arguing over how the guy (Nick) didn't know how to take (Lacey) on a proper date and treat her right and that she (Lacey) wanted him (Nick) to go take a hike (in so many words). They were so boisterous that I could even hear about some other girl (Samantha) and how he was allegedly dating both of them at the same time.

"I'm getting off at this stop. I hope you go and rot in Brooklyn," Lacey yelled as the train warned her to "Stand clear of the closing doors."

The guy across from me had the right idea looking at fun things on his phone and pumping music he actually wanted to listen to into his ears to drown out the unnecessary noise. Headphones were definitely on my list of things to invest in. Sometimes silence is absolutely necessary for the mind to be in tune.

With all the sounds surrounding me, I had completely forgotten that I needed to call my dad back. By the time I arrived at my apartment and walked through the threshold, all I could hear was laughter from Regina and her law school friends, drinking wine while sitting on pillows on the floor (still no couch), and pretending to study some laws or whatever it is they do in law school. I politely said hello and hurried off to my room and closed the door. Somehow, I couldn't escape the noise. I heard giggling and chuckling and laughing and every few minutes someone kept asking, "Who wants more wine?" It was a different voice every time. Apparently my auditory senses had been heightened somewhere along the line of my day. That didn't matter though; I couldn't think. Earlier in the day, I had been seriously contemplating a sort of change in career although I had no career. I was considering the thought that perhaps marketing wasn't the direction I wanted to focus my life into. I didn't know. I only went into the internship at J.A.M. because a) it paid, b) it was something career driven to do, c) it would appease my parents and allow me to move out of the house like they so graciously requested, and d) it paid.

My mind was turning to mush. I had no focus. I hadn't read a new book in over a week, which was a crime against my own humanity. Confusion overwhelmed me and so I collapsed back first into my bed, which was still decorated in princess style. I hadn't yet graduated to more adult bedding. For the time being, I was still perfectly content with denying a part of my adulthood. Sure, I was paying my own bills and "working," but I felt like growing up was for squares and I didn't want to be something that could be easily labeled on a box.

Then, I remembered that I had to return my father's phone call. The last time I had a real conversation with my parents about more than what I was eating and how the internship was and when they could see me next was maybe a month ago – two weeks ago at the very least. Days and weeks were turning into a big blur. I picked up my loud, embarrassing dumb phone and called my dad. He sounded so happy to actually hear my voice instead of getting two-word responses via text message.

"How are things in New York City?" he inquired.

"They're fine. I'm getting used to the subway trains and figuring out where things are."

"Are you having fun? Seeing the sights? Have you seen any celebrities yet?"

"Well, I've been really busy with the internship and all, so I haven't had a whole lot of opportunities to do the touristy things. Besides, I live here now so I'm not a tourist anymore right? Oh, but I thought I saw Jennifer Aniston in a Starbucks the other day, but it wasn't her," I said.

"You should really get out there more. You're only 21 once, right?"

"Right. So what was it that you called me about? That call interrupted the entire office, you know."

"I apologize," my dad rarely apologizes. This was a turning point in itself. "I called to tell you that your mother and I are moving."

"Say what?" I asked skeptically.

"I mean that your mother and I are moving out of the house," he said matter of factly.

"What do you mean?! Where are you moving to?! Are you moving to another house in Bellcastle?"

"No. We're not moving nearby. Actually, we're moving to Puerto Rico."

I paused for a few moments to absorb what I had just heard. *My parents are moving to Puerto Rico? Puerto Rico?! What?!*

"Okay," I responded. "Well. Um. Okay. So. You're leaving me here?! Alone?!"

"Josefina, this is not some plan to leave you in New York City. That is not our intention. We have been thinking about doing this for a while now. It just happens that we found a house there. It's near your *abuela*'s house. You know she needs some help since she's getting older."

"Is that supposed to make me feel better?"

"I'm not trying to upset you. We just don't need all that space in the house anymore with you living in New York. It doesn't make any sense for us."

"And Puerto Rico makes sense?!"

"You know your mother has been wanting to find a place on the island. She's mentioned that for years."

"Yeah, but this is coming out of nowhere. Like, all of a sudden you guys get some spark of inspiration to move to *La Isla del Encanto*? How does this make any sense? Please, humor me."

"Remember how we gave you a time frame to move out on your own and find a career job of some sort so you could sustain yourself?" he started to explain. "This was actually the reason why. We wanted you to be self-sufficient and independent before we left."

"No. No. No," I refused to let any of this information settle in my brain. The longer it stayed there, the more it would feel real. My parents were moving. Moving out of the house I grew up in. Moving outside of the states of the United States and off to an island. Sure, it was still part of the United States, but it was still so far from New York City. I also couldn't understand how my parents could do that to me. They were just going to abandon land and their daughter simultaneously. I just couldn't believe what I was hearing. The synapses in my brain suggested that this was just some twisted dream a.k.a nightmare and that none of this was real. I had to pinch myself to prove it; it hurt.

"Are you still there, Josefina?"

"What? Oh, yeah. I'm still here figuring out how you could do this to me!"

"Okay, stop with the dramatics and the guilt trip. I'm sorry you're having a hard time with this news, *mijita*, honey, but this is a new reality. We're all going to have to get used to it."

"When is this happening? When are you leaving?" I asked, fighting back tears.

"Our stuff will ship out on November 3rd, but our flight is November 1st. It's coming up pretty soon."

"What are you going to do with my stuff? The stuff I left behind."

"We can't take it all with us, so if you want any of your old things from home, you'll have to come and get them before we leave. Your old toys will be donated if you don't want them."

"What about the swing-set-jungle-gym-apparatus?" I asked eagerly.

"We're going to have to leave that old thing in the yard. I'm sorry," he was on a roll with the apologies.

I insisted that this was a hoax and requested my mother's voice on the phone. She told me that they had actually been thinking about this move for a while. They were just waiting for a good time to break the news. It got to the point that I was sick of hearing apologies like, "I'm sorry this," and "I'm sorry that." Nothing they could say would make this situation better in my mind. However, as much as I wanted to be angry and bitter over this decision that was completely tearing me apart inside, I knew I had to come to terms with the fact things in my life were changing. I was changing. My life was changing quickly and I had no way of slowing it down. After about an hour attempting to convince my parents to stay, it occurred to me that they were leaving a few weeks before Thanksgiving and a month and a half before Christmas. What was I going to do for the holidays? None of this was fair.

Part of me wanted to complain about how my life isn't fair. Part of me didn't want to talk about it at all. Part of me wanted to scream. Part of me wanted to roll up in a ball and cry until no more tears would come out. The latter part won over.

CHAPTER FOURTEEN

"It is not so much our friends' help that helps us as the con-
fident knowledge that they will help us." – Epicurus

I was grieving – not over a person necessarily, but over everything I
knew to be good and right in my life: my childhood. Granted it wasn't
completely a youth full of butterflies and rainbows, but I found a way
to hold onto any good memories and discarded the crappy ones. My
parents leaving me behind to move to Puerto Rico for a fresh start on
an island full of coconuts and sunshine seemed selfish at first. Upon
further examination of how they pushed me to move out of my childhood home as a way to help me grow up before their tropical depar-
ture, I started to come to terms with these new changes in my life. The
whole "Get a Job and Move to Manhattan" project seemed to me as
only a temporary situation, as if I could return to the bedroom I spent
21 pretty decent years of my life in any day now. None of this seemed
permanent. I was starting to realize that more and more, this was real.
I could pull off every trick in the book – temper tantrums, silent treatment, running away – but none of those would help in this case. Left
to my own devices, I was forced to accept a new reality, yet again, and
grow up a little bit more.

When Regina's law school friends left our apartment for the night,
she came and found me in my room where I sat on my bed with my
arms around my bent knees with my face lodged between the crevice

between my legs. She attempted to coerce me from that position, but I wouldn't budge. I hoped that if I ignored her for long enough, Regina would give up and leave my bedroom.

Regina stayed in my room. Actually, after figuring out that I wasn't going to spill the beans so easily on why I had mentally and physically shut down, she left for a minute to grab a magazine and then returned to sit at the foot of my bed flipping through the pages. It was one of those extra thick issues of a fashion magazine that could keep her occupied for hours.

"Oh my God! This dress is so cute, right?" Regina showed my curled up body the magazine spread, but I didn't even glance at it to enthuse her.

Still, she continued to try to entice a smile out of me and get me talking. She just loved to hear the latest gossip. It was in her nature.

"You know, Josefina, you can't stay silent forever about whatever is bothering you. It's just not healthy. Like when Roy and I get into a fight, I always *try* to keep quiet. Limit the talking, you know? But then he'll say something stupid and I'll get really angry and then it's just an explosive mess."

After a whole 60 seconds of silence, I said from inside the cave my body had created for itself, "I know. I'm usually here when the mess happens."

"Yeah. Well, we always make up. I can't stay mad at my Roy for too long," Regina said. "Don't you and Malcolm ever fight about anything?"

"Not really," I muttered.

"You don't fight about anything? I find that hard to believe."

I slowly lifted my head from its collapsed position, said, "No. We don't fight," and then quickly returned to my less than upright position almost like a Hungry Hungry Hippo would open its mouth, catch as many little white balls as it could and return to its original closed off, default stance. I had become a hippo. What's worse was I was actually getting hungry. Grieving my childhood was stirring up my appetite.

After making my way past Regina, who was still clearly confused about my sudden depressed state, yet still completely engrossed in her magazine, I went to the kitchen to scrounge around for some food. All I found in my cupboard was a half-eaten box of chocolate chip cookies. My shelf in the fridge had just enough milk for a milk and cookies session, which is exactly what happened. I brought the milk and cookies to my bedroom, where Regina was still flipping through pages of the encyclopedia-sized magazine.

"You want to talk? Okay. Let's talk," I said directly. "My parents are going to Puerto Rico."

"Like on vaycay? Cool! Are you going with them?"

"No. It's not cool and no, I'm not going with them. Let me rephrase: My parents are *moving* to Puerto Rico. Like, permanently."

"Oh my God! No way! Now I see why you were acting like a hermit," Regina said.

"They're leaving the first week of November, which is coming up soon so I have to say goodbye to all my old stuff from my childhood, which is killing me."

"Why is it killing you? It's just old stuff from when you were, like, five."

My eyes narrowed on her and I gave her the stink-eye – the only non-verbal comeback I could muster up.

"Clearly, you don't know me very well. That *stuff* isn't just stuff to me. That *stuff* made me happy when I was a kid. There were my dolls and games and books. They were all integral parts of my childhood. They made me who I am today, which is still a work in progress, but I'm okay with that. I think. And my swing-set-jungle-gym-apparatus is staying with the house so the new owners can rip her out of the ground and throw it away. You have no idea what that stuff means to me and now all I'll have are distant memories of all of that *stuff*!" I paused for a moment to wipe the tears that were erupting from my eyes. "And what's worse is that I don't know if advertising and marketing or public relations are what I want to be doing at all. I feel like I'm on a completely wrong path now and I don't know what to do. I don't know what I want to be when I grow up. I envy the people who already know they want to be doctors and lawyers and teachers and computer people. It's so unfair. Why can't I just inherently know what and who I want to be?" Cookie break. "And I've been so busy that I haven't had a chance to call Bethany in months. She's my best, best, bestest friend. And then Malcolm is really great, but I feel like I never have time to hang out with him anymore. I've gotten so caught up with interning at J.A.M. that I haven't had enough blocks of time to spend with him. And he's probably going to break up with me for it," I wiped some more tears from my face. "I wouldn't blame him for it either. I don't know how to be a girlfriend. I've never had a boyfriend before. This is all so new to me and I'm losing it. I'm losing my mind and soon I'm going to be losing my family to *La Isla del Encanto* and I'm going to be alone here in this big city."

I helped myself to some more cookies and milk. It was absolutely necessary. As I dug into the box of delicious chocolate chip cookies, Regina simply looked at me as if she were trying to find the right words to say. She made some attempts to construct a sentence that could potentially make me feel better. Though she tried to be a comforting friend, she had a bit of a hard time vocalizing those words of comfort.

"I know you can't take all of your stuff from your parents' house, but maybe you could keep one thing – like your favorite thing – for old times sake," she suggested.

"Impossible. I can't bring it here."

"What do you mean? It can't be that hard to bring a dollhouse or something here, you know."

"My favorite thing from home is my swing-set-jungle-gym-apparatus and –"

"I'm sorry. Your 'apparatus' what now?" Regina interrupted with a confused look slapped across her face.

"My swing-set-jungle-gym-apparatus. It's my old swing set. My dad set it up in the backyard when I was seven. Since then, it's been my play place and my thinking place. I always think better up in the air suspended by the seat. And I don't care how old I am, if there's a swing set somewhere and I can actually play on it, there's no way I'm not going to go play on it. It's a relic, but it's my favorite relic on that property and in a few weeks, it's going to belong to some other family. Or worse – they might tear it down and install a new fangled swing-set-jungle-gym-apparatus, but they won't call it that. It would just be a swing set or a jungle gym to them. It would mean nothing. It's the end of an era," I explained my plight.

"I'll say! You're getting all choked up about a swing set – excuse me – swing-set-jungle-gym-apparatus. Clearly there is a lot of sentimental value in this thing and you guys go way back, but you are 21 years old now! Seriously. You need to stop mourning a swing set and your childhood for that matter. It's not healthy, Josefina."

Regina snapped me into a new reality that I knew was bound to catch up with me. Was I really mourning my childhood? Was it time to put on my big girl pants already? Somewhere in my brain, I thought that moving to New York City on my own and getting real work experience would help me grow up. I always expected things to happen instantaneously like POOF and whatever I desired would appear or POOF and whatever problem I had would disappear. Life is not like a magic trick.

After Regina left my grieving self alone in my room, I grabbed my cell phone from the Stone Age and called Bethany. Even though we only had a one year difference in age, it seemed to me that Bethany matured faster than I did. She also knew me better than anyone I could call at the moment.

"Josefina!" Bethany squealed on the other end. "Took you long enough to call. I was starting to think you were perpetually underground in the subway tunnels and couldn't get a call out from not having any service. What's going on?"

After explaining the whole situation about my parents moving to an island that wasn't Manhattan, my swing-set-jungle-gym-apparatus problems, and how I was miserable at J.A.M., which was a brave thing to do considering Bethany's father was a head honcho there, she took pause.

"Well, that's a lot of stuff on the table. Why didn't you tell me about all of this sooner? I mean, that's what best friends are for," Bethany said.

"I would have told you three hours ago when all of these issues smacked me in the face, but you know me, I had a silent treatment pity party to drown my sorrows."

"Ah yes. I am familiar with that coping mechanism. It's a little fourth grade if you ask me," she joked, but I knew she was dead serious.

Why was everyone and everything in the universe telling me that I was getting too old to play games? People play games on their Smartphones on the train all the time. It seemed like some sort of double standard was impeding on my Peter Pan complex. I was a forever-kid through and through. Who decided the age where it's too old to be too young anyway?

"I'm completely aware that sometimes I act like I'm in fourth grade. Trust me, I know. I just feel like it's affecting me at my internship and I'm sure it's putting a strain on my relationship with Malcolm," I said.

"Have you told Malcolm about all of this yet?"

"No…" I said with a guilty conscience.

Bethany's prescription was to call Malcolm and tell him all about the situations that just recently and quickly became black holes disturbing my brain. She said that my parents wouldn't have made the decision to move to Puerto Rico if they didn't think I could handle things on the mainland myself. She also suggested I hold out for a while longer on the internship at J.A.M. Considering I still needed money to live in New York, it made sense to stay. And in the meantime, I could try to find another career path that would make me happy.

"You're gonna be okay, Josie. These are just some growing pains, but remember, you're a forever-kid. Getting a little more mature won't take that away. It's just in who you are," Bethany said some of the wisest words I had ever heard her speak.

I had gotten in the habit of exclusively texting Malcolm. Actual phone calls were rare. I would only hear his voice when we would go to dinner on Thursday nights or if we went out with Georgina, the wild child, on an occasional Saturday night. Our relationship was getting strained and I knew I needed to be the one to reach out to try and make it better. I decided to take some inspiration from some of my favorite Rom-Coms and make a grand romantic gesture so hopefully he would be reminded of how gorgeous and charming I was (a minor exaggeration) and why he liked me from the beginning. I was desperately trying to avoid a breakup. He was my first boyfriend ever and he was pretty good at it, considering my aloofness and naïveté. Also, with my parents fleeing my homeland for theirs, I needed all the good friends I could find more than ever.

It was late and I was not fond of going out in New York City alone at night, but there was something important I needed to do and I needed to be brave about it. I pulled on a jacket and headed outside of my building in the direction of the subway station on Delancey Street. Surprised by how cold it was, I hurried past the shops and people on the streets. Finally, I got to the subway station and somehow found comfort in the stinky warmth of the underground air. The train arrived and I was on my way uptown on my own official business. After nine stops on the train, I got off and headed toward my destination, still being overly careful not to get mugged or end up in some neighborhood I really didn't want to be in. I also didn't want to get lost because being lost in New York City at night was not exactly my idea of a good time. Manhattan streets look different at night than they do in the daytime. Eventually, I made it to my destination. I looked over the names corresponding with the buzzers for the building. I was looking for Dodson. *Dodson, Dodson, Dodson,* I thought as I eyed the list of residents. Then, it jumped out at me though I had already passed over it about four times. I pushed the button a few times reflecting my impatience and obnoxiousness.

"Who goes there?" a cracked sounding voice was amplified over the intercom. It was the nerdiest intercom greeting I had ever heard.

"It's Josefina! Is Malcolm home?" I yelled at the speaker so loud the people in the apartments on the second floor could probably hear me.

"Yeah, he's here. Come on up," the unidentified voice said and buzzed me into the building.

I made my way up to the fifth floor, where Malcolm lived with Roy and his other roommate that I had never met. By the time I reached their door, I was out of breath and needed to lean against a wall for a moment to regain my composure. Those were steep stairs. I didn't want to knock on the door and look like the hot mess that I was. I needed to look as put together as that day we met on the train going into Penn Station; the point was to remind him of how great I was before I became a workaholic.

After I wiped the sweat from my forehead and smoothed out my hair, I stumbled up to Malcolm's door and knocked furiously. I held onto the doorframe to hold myself up. He opened the door wearing a T-shirt that read, "I Live Dangerously." That was quite a hyperbolic statement, but I realized sometimes it's okay to aspire to hyperbolic statements.

He stared at me and his mouth formed a smile. "Hi there, stranger," he said sweetly.

"Yeah. I know I've been all over the place lately. I'm sorry."

"Did you come all the way up here on your own? I know you hate going out at night in the city by yourself."

"I did. I realized I can't be afraid of the dark forever," I admitted. "The thing is, I really need a friend tonight. Things are going kind of crazy all of a sudden and I need you."

"Well, we can talk about it in the hall like this, or we can talk in here, where it's only slightly more private," Malcolm laughed a little and I giggled in response. "Roy and Dave are in the kitchen, hence *slightly* more private than the hall."

I stepped inside and turned to the kitchen, where Roy and Dave (so that was his name!) were snacking on Doritos and Oreo cookies. "Enjoy the fine dining, boys."

Malcolm and I sat down on his futon in the living room and I told him about all my family and career troubles. He was the only one I knew I could talk to without feeling judged. It felt like a therapy session or something with all the tears. I was on the verge of swearing a few times, but something in my lexicon wouldn't allow me to go to that extreme. My parents raised me in a non-swearing household. Sometimes I could get away with swearing in Spanish, but I would still usually get in trouble. I learned to just not go there. So I made up alternative words like, "oh, French toast," or "you son of a baby diaper." My mother still found those offensive, but I used them anyway.

"Do you have any other family nearby?" Malcolm asked me.

153

I only had an aunt on my mother's side who lived in Colorado, which wasn't exactly the easiest place to get to just to have coffee on a Saturday morning or something. Besides, I had only met her once when I was, like, four. All I had left here were my friends, but I was back to the drawing board with career prospects and although I had friends, I still felt completely lost and alone.

Malcolm gave me a hug and said, "I'm still here. You know that."

"But I've been such a son of a baby diaper to you lately," I said while I was still in his arms.

"A 'son of a' what?"

"Um, don't worry about it. It's just a … it's nothing," I shrugged it off.

"I really like you, Josefina. I like spending time with you."

"When I have time to spend with you," I joked.

"Yeah. I really hope we can make this work together," Malcolm said as he wiped a tear from my cheek. You've been really stressed lately and now I see what's on your plate. No one said life in New York would be easy. It can be lonely and harsh sometimes, but at least you know I'm your friend – not only your boyfriend."

"I've always wanted one of those," I said with a teary-eyed smile.

Malcolm wiped a tear from my cheek and kissed me at that spot. We paused the conversation for a moment and just looked at each other in the eyes. I was pretty sure one of us would break the silence that was not at all awkward. While attempting to conjure up some clever and completely inappropriate words to say, Malcolm spoke.

"I love you, Josefina," he said without breaking eye contact.

He held my hands together for a second and observed my reaction, which was one of utter shock. This was uncharted territory. I had never said, "I love you," to anyone besides people in my family. I hadn't even kissed anyone romantically before Malcolm came along. He introduced me to a New York I never knew existed – one in which the nightly news on TV had often characterized the city as one full of darkness and doom. Malcolm showed me the beauties of Manhattan that newscasters had clearly overlooked time and time again. Regardless, Malcolm had just told me he loves me. I should have had a knee-jerk reaction to those three words that one would expect from a girl like me. But my immediate response to his outpouring of emotion was an easy one. At least it was supposed to be.

"Malcolm, you are quite possibly the one person I've met who has helped me adjust to this whole transition period more than anyone. You didn't force me to grow up so quickly without giving me time to process everything. You met me on a New Jersey Transit train and helped me get to my interview – because you and I both know I would have gotten lost and ended up on Staten Island or something. When I came to New York for our day of fun exploring the city, you took me to all the places that somehow, you knew I would enjoy (even in the blistering heat). I didn't know anything about romantic relationships other than what I learned from Drew Barrymore movies. And that's kind of how I operate. Some people call it Peter Pan syndrome. Bethany calls me a forever-kid. Somehow, some way, you've found a way to embrace my inner forever-kid and not get completely sick of me. Now I've never told anyone I love them in a romantic sense before. This is all still really new to me. That being said, one wise philosopher named Plato once wrote that, "Love is a serious mental disease." I think that was pretty accurate because it is contagious and I love you, too." I finally said in one swift shot. "I realize I've been talking a lot–"

That was when Malcolm went in for a big kiss and pulled me close to him in his arms. Passionate and sweet, it felt like a cathartic moment for both of us. His romantic gesture caught me by surprise in that I was surprised not having been in a boyfriend-girlfriend relationship before. Then I remembered all of those dramatic kisses in all of the Rom-Coms I watched religiously as official handbooks to life and love, so I kissed him back and followed whatever he was doing. I was an adult in training and needed someone to hold my hand and help me jump to the next stage of my life.

CHAPTER FIFTEEN

"Man is most nearly himself when he achieves the
seriousness of a child at play." - Heraclitus

Change sometimes comes in stages. Sometimes change comes in one brutal gust of wind. The question is if we will allow the change to affect us, change us, and make us better, or if we will remain unchanged in the face of it. Is it better to evolve rather than remain the same despite the forces that are bound to change the playing field of life? I spent a lot of time contemplating this idea and I started to understand. Even though I may have been called a forever-kid and resisted change as though it were the worst thing to ever affect my life, I knew that I could only stay the same for so long. Honestly, I was beginning to be aware of the fact that being unchanged was only convenient until the elements come into play, influencing one to make a choice. It was always difficult for me to make definitive choices about my life. In fact, even as a child, it was a challenge to decide between the Barbie Jeep or the Barbie swimming pool at the toy store. But I was no longer in a position for picking doll accessories. I was growing up and I needed to adjust and become more accustomed to making big decisions about my life. At this point, more than ever, I needed to gain control of my life. Sure, I had made big changes, but before I was forced to solve actual problems in my life on my own, I was completely fine with my lifestyle. After all, I never had to take real responsibility over any important situations. That's what my mom and dad were there for. With them leaving my childhood home that we lived in together for 21 years, I came to realize that they had found a way to make a life change that in turn, pushed me to grow up. While they were rather overprotective of me for all of those years under their roof, it was their way of letting me be a kid while I still could.

I lived a haphazard life for 21 years and I was prepared for it to continue to be haphazard for at least another 21. I went through a growth spurt of sorts. It was painful and uncomfortable, dramatic and heart-wrenching, and frustrating beyond belief. However, none of those adjectives that impeded the way I *thought* my life would go (as if I had a plan in the first place) could break my spirit. No one was as surprised as I was that I took the avocados I was given and made a relatively decent guacamole.

One thing always encouraged my forever-kid philosophy: my swing-set-jungle-gym-apparatus. Within the rusted metal structure with fading painted stripes were all of my secrets. It was like therapy in the form of a swing. It weathered my ups and downs, and transformed my lonely existence into a world of laughter and play. Despite all of the trials and tribulations of the past year, leaving that hunk of metal in the ground on the last day my parents would live in my childhood home was the toughest. And I was never good at goodbyes. I remember one particular Christmas party that my parents threw. The guests would arrive with gifts (my favorite part), mingle, and eat some dinner. By the time everyone was ready to go on their merry way, it was time for good-byes. My mother would encourage me to be polite and sociable. I was seven years old. Polite I could handle, but asking me to be "sociable" was a different story. Rather than follow my mother's orders, I would either a) hide behind her, b) run up to my room to hide, or c) take off to my swing-set-jungle-gym-apparatus (sometimes with a winter coat) as a sort of oddly-shaped security blanket. It never occurred to me that eventually I would have to say goodbye to it.

So with tears welling up in my eyes to the point that I couldn't hold them back any longer, I hopped on my swing set for the final time.

"Hey there, old friend," I said, caressing the slightly rusted chain links that held the seat in mid-air.

I looked around at the bald spot in the lawn under the swing where my feet had grazed the grass so many times that it stopped growing. The new owners of the house would probably fill that in. I took my shoes off for old time sake.

My swing set was a relic – memorabilia of a time past. I pushed off with my bare feet and started slowly. I wanted to relish every second. Then, I decided that for my last ride, I wanted to feel like a child again. I wanted to be that seven year old who wore weird pink glasses, rarely got Valentine's Day cards in school, and was labeled a dweeb every day of elementary school. I still couldn't let go of these sore spots in my life, but Bethany was right; I was a forever-kid. Wherever I went, I managed to find that seven year old version of Josefina inside myself and let the world celebrate that side of me. Mr. Jenkins seemed to find it as an invaluable asset to his advertising team. Apparently, Malcolm found it to be a rather endearing quality that he simply couldn't get enough of. I liked to think it kept my parents feeling young. And I guess Bethany liked the idea of it as well. She was turning 24 and to her, that was more terrifying than finding a tiny spider on a wall. I was lucky to be a forever-kid. It meant that while I was growing up in certain ways, I would always have a little bit of that childlike energy, humor, and perspective that most people abandon after turning 13. Being a forever-kid was embedded in my DNA. It was a quality no one could take away from me. And while this swing-set-jungle-gym-apparatus was something that could indeed be taken away from me, the feeling of the breeze on my face and in between my toes could never be forgotten.

"Josefina, it's time to go," I could hear my mother calling for me.

I slowed the swing to a stop and lingered for a moment, knowing this would be the end of an era. Placing my feet firmly on the ground weathered by 21 years of playtime and stepping away from the swing was possibly the hardest part. I wasn't sure I was ready to let go of my childlike sensibilities and go forth into the world as an adult without a security blanket back home. My hands refused to release my grip on the chain links. Eventually, after a few more minutes essentially grieving over my swing-set-jungle-gym-apparatus, I let go.

Walking away was an action of moving forward. I wasn't turning my back on any aspect of my life. It was more than that. It was always about more than just a swing set. It was something bigger than that. It was about growing up no matter how up things were or how down it got. Most importantly, I learned that in life, there will always be an upswing.

ABOUT THE AUTHOR

Adriana Erin Rivera is a twenty-five-year-old writer living in Hoboken, New Jersey. She has studied Advertising and Marketing Communications at the Fashion Institute of Technology. Her writing has been published in the *New York Metro* newspaper, *Latina Magazine,* and *Footwear News.* *Swing Sets* is her first novel.

www.adrianaerinrivera.com